KORAKI

George Ploumidis

Ένα περιστέρι δεν έχει θέση ανάμεσα στα κοράκια

A dove has no place among crows - Greek proverb

The silent thoughts of a full church converged on the man in the open coffin. Nectarios Petrakis, two days short of his sixty-third birthday, lay pale, his once olive skin desaturated. Though in truth, he had been pale for some time. He looked so much smaller in this final pose – in proportion, but smaller. Nicola kissed his Father's forehead, just as his Father kissed him from infancy right through to adulthood. He resisted the urge to rush and be efficient. He lingered until he was ready to move back to his position in the front row.

Nicola scanned Ayios Yiannis. The non-Greeks in the church were easy to spot from the less austere colour of their clothing. The Greeks were dressed in mournful black, *mavro*. A *mavro* of Greeks thought Nicola, a fitting collective noun for Greeks at a funeral. He tried to think of things other than what was right in front of him, but this was not the time for daydreaming. The chandelier above the casket throbbed in and out with his pulse and sweat amassed on his forehead like an army ready to attack. Eyes passed over him, the Archangels watching from every angle then merging into one hybrid figure, his breathing now short and shallow. The Priest's robes lifted like eagle's wings as he implored that the deceased's memory be kept eternal. Nicola grabbed at the seat in front of him, the metal clang attracting attention from the congregation and a cautionary glance from the Priest, who continued without missing a beat. A squeeze of his shoulder from his uncle Claudio brought

him back. He gripped his uncle for balance as he took a
seat. It was a while before he could bring himself to meet
the sympathetic gazes and double kisses of the sea of
friends and relatives he hadn't seen for years.

Nicola took a sip of water and patted his face dry. He
motioned to his cousins, Pari and Aki to join him and
Claudio to carry the casket out of the church.

Nicola stopped. *Almost forgot.* He reached into his
pocket and placed a small plastic zip lock bag under
Nectarios' crossed hands. It took no small amount of
patience to wait for his Mother to fall asleep so he could
snip off some of her hair that Nectarios asked to take
with him. With a final glance, he crossed himself and
nodded as a sign to close the casket.

They carried Nectarios to the hearse, the sun giving way
to a sudden cool change and the
rude spit of moisture. The movement of wind was a relief
to Nicola after the stuffy, claustrophobic church.

Some mourners attended to their phones. Some sought
cover from the impending rain, and some accosted
people they only saw in times of joy or tragedy. Others
simply willed the process to end so they could return to
their own world. He suppressed the urge to judge and
kept his posture straight.

Time passed in a haze, and the next thing Nicola knew he
was in the car with Claudio as they followed the hearse.

"Bravo, Nicola. Bastardi turning up, pretending to care. Not even one in ten knew him."

Who really knows anyone? thought Nicola. Nectarios' final six months filtered the real friends from the fair-weather ones. Even some of his closest friends opted out towards the end, finding the sight of him withering too much to bear. And worst of all, for the last six months of his life, Lidia, his wife of nearly 40 years didn't even recognise him.

"We'll go see your Mother after, yes?"

"Si, Zio."

At the burial, people huddled under umbrellas in a horseshoe pattern around the plot. Clumps of dirt pattered against the casket as one mourner after another completed the holy ritual. Nicola grabbed a handful and hesitated. He wanted to thump it hard against the coffin, but instead, he caressed the cold lump of earth in his hands. Finally, he dropped it, his hand almost numb. His focus moved to the grassed plot next to Nectarios, where Lidia would one day re-join him.

Walking back to the car, it started. Whispers in Greek, Italian and English. Different languages, same questions.

Will he sell the house?
Which one, he had lots of property you know, even a factory.
How much?

Is the plot next to him for Lidia?

On and on. Italians and Greeks were una faccia, una razza – 'one face, one race', all consumed by the lives of others as much as their own. The formalities over, they couldn't fucking help themselves. Rumours about the property Nectarios owned spread like the cancer that consumed him. Nicola accepted there would be gossip, but five seconds after the burial? They could have at least waited until he was out of earshot before carrying on. Speaking both languages was an unwanted gift at times. Basta. Enough.

Gossip and the persistent rain made Nicola's right cheekbone itch. Knock it on the head, he told himself. He strode to the front of the group, mopped the damp hair out of his eyes, turned back and faced everyone.

"Thank you for coming to pay your respects. I am grateful. There will be no wake."

He walked back through the group and thanked the Priest. He looked down the hole where his Father lay, the rain falling a little heavier and collecting at the edges. He wiped his feet on the grass and mouthed 'Goodbye, Nectario', crossing himself, before trudging to the car on his own.

Nicola chose the Santa Croce Nursing Home not on finances, meal plans, good hygiene, activities, or the staff's bedside manner, but on a gut feeling. Located in Heidelberg, it was further away than the other homes on his shortlist. This one felt good. His Mother Lidia always told him to trust his instincts. Sempre il primo istinto, Nicola! Owner Marco Fontolan's Mother also received care for dementia there.

Lidia waved to Nicola and Claudio as they appeared in the doorway, her greying hair tied back. Her skin had lost some of its tone, but her dimples and cheekbones remained untouched. She swung her legs onto the floor and hugged her son and brother, the strength belying her petite form. Nicola hadn't seen her this alert in weeks. Her eyes, greyer some months ago, now gleamed aquamarine again. Oh God, he thought, then admonished himself for fearing the worst. He should have been happy to see her smile. She backed away and inspected the duo.

Lidia's smile was replaced by a puzzled look and she glanced from Claudio's jacket to Nicola's, then out the window, where blue sky replaced the rain. The men searched for an explanation for their wet, formal clothing.

Lidia turned and met Nicola's eyes.

"Perche cosi formali?"

"Signora Aurelia died from a stroke." said Nicola to Claudio's relief. This was true – but the Aurelia in question died a few weeks back.

"Aurelia! Che povera."

Nicola reflected that he and Claudio were the last links to Lidia's past. Every time he visited his Mother he wondered if this time she would finally ask where her husband was. She knew Nicola was her son, but somehow, she never asked to fill the gap about her husband. Dr Fredel, the home's gerontologist, put it down to the fickle nature of dementia.

Broaching the topic of Nectarios was, in short, impossible. Having to explain to Lidia that she was once married, and her husband died of cancer was too hard. Fredel advised against reconstructing this history for her. It could send her falling off whatever stable patch of ground her mind occupied at the time. Nicola felt guilty that this made things easier for him, but he saw sense in it. She was still labile and prone to huge mood swings. Managing her dementia and Cluster A personality was like spinning plates. She could be engaging on Sunday, aggressive on Monday, and listless on Tuesday. Today was a good day.

Claudio played it safe. "What are they feeding you?"

"Yesterday it was cacciatore. Schifo," she said, screwing up her face.

Cacciatore, polpetti, risotto, osso buco, lasagne, arancini. Every dish was a Lidia specialty, her cooking filling the house with aromas. In a cruel joke, she now tolerated someone else's cooking with a heightened sense of smell and taste.

They ate and broke bread like many times before dementia stole the Lidia they knew. After lunch, they went for a short walk through the garden. Lidia soon became drowsy. They tucked her in and she bid them ciao through weary lids.

On the way out, Nicola waved at Marco. He was busy handling two phone lines and a family arguing in the foyer. A familiar scene was playing out, an elderly Father surrounded by three imploring, middle aged children trying to sell the idea to him. The Father argued with each in turn, unwilling to accept his fate.

"C'e puzza della morte. No, no e no!" It smells of death.

On any other day, Nicola would have stopped to chat with them. Children and parents swapping roles was one of life's harshest turning points. Claudio turned, his face a road map of wrinkles. His resemblance to Paulie Walnuts from *The Sopranos* was uncanny. Only the silver wing tips were missing.

"Grazie, Nicola. I thought the game was down."

"You mean the game was up."

"You know what I mean."

The irritations of Bell St peppered the drive to Claudio's house in North Coburg. "Vaffanculo stronzo!" yelled Claudio from the passenger seat with a side of hand gestures. Nicola laughed. Italians had more crude hand signals than pasta varieties. Greeks kept it simple with the solitary open-palm moutza, efficient and universal.

"You laugh, eh? Let's see how tolerant you are at my age."

Nicola dropped Claudio off with a hug.

"Come in for a bit."

"I'm going to get some rest."

"Rest here. You need it."

"Thanks, but I'm tired. I'll go home."

"Va bene, go home and get some rest."

The rain pelted down as Nicola opened the front gate. He ran to the front door, only to find containers of food and cakes stacked neatly in front of it. Food served Greeks and Italians well in any emotional state. Carrying the last of it down the hallway, he caught his reflection in the full-length mirror by the door. Lidia insisted on having it there for a last-minute check before leaving the house.

His body looked thin – if he hadn't steeled himself
against self-pity, he might even have said gaunt.
There was food for that.
He started on the spanakorizo and followed up with roast
lamb, potatoes and zucchini. For dessert, he tossed up
between bougatsa and tiramisu, soon deciding on a bit of
both. After a quick round of fridge tetris, he found room
for everything.

Despite its clean edges and surfaces, the fresh, three-
year-old kitchen looked anaemic without the traffic.
Whenever Lidia cooked, Nectarios would sneak up and
steal a sample with his heatproof hands. The smack of
the wooden spoon inevitably followed, Nectarios'
pickpocket laugh ringing down the hallway.

Belly full, Nicola trod off to bed. His watch said 5.35
p.m., but he wanted to draw a line under the day.

3

Sleep came the moment his head hit the pillow. Synapses had other ideas, springing into action, like a zoo of nocturnal creatures summoned from the undergrowth.

Snakes, two of them raced towards Nicola. He stared and tensed up at the sound of them tussling. The larger, more muscular snake crushed its smaller opponent. Like metal twisting, buckling, then giving way. The victor presented its oversized head and slippery brown torso to Nicola, the losing snake a jumble of distorted pieces.

The dominant snake shattered into pixels, reformed ten metres away into a fluid, metallic form and burrowed out of sight into soft sand.

Then came a second dream, a familiar one from his childhood.

A murder of crows perched on the roof above his parents' bedroom. The roof slick with rain reflected the afternoon sun, the crows' edges blurred with light. The crows aarked in unison until the leader stretched his wings and they flew away.

Drinking his macchiato thirteen hours later, Nicola pursed his lips. He knew as a clinical psychologist that some dreams were the subconscious having its time. The rest were random chemistry, short clips unworthy of classification.

The crows were real. Lidia's older cousin Stefano visited
when Nicola was eight. One afternoon, two crows
perched on the guttering above Stefano's room. Nicola
noticed them again as he left for school the next morning
and were there again as he got home. On the third night,
Stefano got up for a drink of water. He bumped into a
chair in the kitchen and woke Nicola. He watched him
walk back down the narrow hallway, heard the flush of
the toilet then sleep. He woke to the sound of his Mother
wailing. Nectarios held her back as paramedics tried to
revive Stefano. Dead at fifty-one from a heart attack.

4

Nicola met Iain Grafton at ten a.m. for the reading of the will, the office bordered with the same wood panelling since 1973. He handled each of Nectarios' real estate purchases and was well trusted by his Father. A tall, gangly man, Grafton laid out the documents on his enormous desk. There wasn't a computer in sight, just neat piles of documents stacked like buildings.

Nectarios nominated Grafton as the executor of the will and only wanted Nicola present for the reading. He reeled off the assets in a dry tone. As sole heir, Nicola inherited a large property portfolio; the family home in Station Street, North Carlton, houses in Richmond, Northcote, Clifton Hill, North Fitzroy and an enormous factory on Albert Street, Preston.

"These are all paid off and rented. Nectarios set up automatic payments for Lidia's care from the combined rental pool. He stressed that this continues as long as required. He also left one-hundred thousand dollars for his sisters Rita and Sia, and your Uncle Claudio. He asked that you talk to each of them separately. He said you would have the good sense not to have a family meeting about it and create a circus. He also left a safety box at the bank. Here's the key. He didn't specify what the contents were."

After signatures and initials, they shook hands. Iain squeezed Nicola's shoulder. He knew him since birth.

"Nicola, your Father was very proud of you." Grafton
looked at the floor and waited for the exchange to pass.

Nicola smiled. "Thanks, Iain."

Stuck between breakfast and lunch and official duties
over with, Nicola decided to visit Nectarios. He drove
home and walked the five minutes. When he looked at
buying twin cemetery plots, Nectarios held back tears.
The thought of Lidia leaving the earth before him shook
his pragmatic business sense. Caught up in this memory,
Nicola lost his bearings. He then recalled seven. Seventh
Avenue winded north, then made a gentle right turn to
run parallel with MacPherson Street. Sia and his
youngest cousin Petra stood by the grave. They looked
up and smiled. The twin rush of hugs almost crushed his
form.

"I called before. Nectarios' voice is still on the answering
machine." said Sia.

Nicola saw the flowers arranged like soldiers guarding
the cross, their symmetry obvious.

"Did you guys arrange these?"

"No, they were like that when we arrived. We thought
you might have done it."

Sia and Petra hugged Nicola goodbye. He tried
connecting with Nectarios' eyes in the photo facing him.
They looked as pale as he did in the casket. Nicola

wondered if photos lost their colour when their subject
left the earth. Rain fell on his grave for a second time,
this time harder and with an obscene angle of attack.
Unprotected, Nicola sprinted under a tree on the shortest
side and waited until a break came, cursing the rain.

5

Rita Stelidis laid out her favourite tablecloth and ran her hand to smooth its tactile weave. Pari and Aki would dash in and breakfast would be ready when they did. Angelo would be up later after his night shift. This gave her a couple of hours after breakfast to catch up with friends for coffee, then a quick grocery run.

Pari ran in and started tucking into his eggs, almost gorging himself into indigestion. Aki stood at the island bench and shook his head at his frenetic brother. They may have been twins, but sharing birthdays was where it stopped. Aki gave his Mum a peck and good morning, before starting his eggs and his weakness of vegemite and cheesy toast.

Through a cluttered mouth, Pari asked his Mother how much property his Uncle Nectarios owned.

"Mind your own business." Rita said.

"It is our business isn't it? How much do you think we'll get?"

"These things never end well," said Aki, pushing his thick fringe from his face.

"What do you mean, Aki?" asked Rita, hands on hips.

"You have the old-world wog entitlement syndrome. He owes me." said Aki, pointing his finger at himself. "I guarantee you, whatever Nicola brings, and it's your brother's wish, not Nicola's, it won't be good enough for you."

Rita slapped the bench. "How do you speak to me like this, Aki? What do you know about obligation?"

"I never mentioned the word obligation. You did. If I am wrong tonight, let me know."

"Aki's never wrong, Mum. Didn't you know?" teased Pari.

"Whatever." said Aki, waving him away.

"I'm done anyway. God forbid I block any of the golden rays you're emitting." Pari dumped his plate and cutlery in the dishwasher and returned to the townhouse he and Aki shared behind his parent's house.

Aki dismissed his brother as impulsive, with his revolving door of girlfriends and inconsistent employment history. He was smart but lacked judgement. But Aki lacked Pari's brashness and drive, and he reflected that a man with their collective positives would be formidable. Such is nature, he thought.

Rita stroke Aki's unkempt hair with a gentle hand.

"I'm sorry, Mum."

"I should tell myself you're twenty-seven more often.
You can have an opinion. This hair, you really should get
it under control it if you won't cut it."

"And use my body weight in gel like Pari?"

"You two are different. Your beauty is up here." she said,
tapping his forehead.

"Gotta go Mum. I've got a lecture to give at midday."

"The PhD, any news?"

"I find out in two or three days."

Rita squeezed Aki's cheeks. "Bravo Aki!"

"A Doctorate is a long process Mum; it has to be peer-
reviewed, submitted and accepted."

"Okay, okay, details. Now you have your own path. Get
married..."

"Have a good day Mum." he said, kissing her on the
cheek. He hated the whole find a girl/get married
conversation but couldn't bring himself to make his
Mother feel bad about it.

Rita sat and thought of Nectarios. They came across
together, she fifteen, Sia six and Nectarios nineteen.
Their parents, Nikos and Fotini died within a year of
moving to Melbourne in a car crash. A drunken driver

ran a red light and killed them both instantly as they left
Victoria Market. Nectarios built their lives up again as a
Father, Mother and brother, steering his sisters through
the grief.

Rita wondered what was coming to her. She and Angelo
weren't hard up, but for Rita, it was a symbolic thing.
She appreciated that Nectarios looked after them when
their parents died, but that was expected in her mind.
Wouldn't any eldest sibling have done the same? She
was still absorbed by these thoughts as she rolled onto
the road without giving way. She missed Mrs Bennett by
inches, earning a hearty honk of the horn and a shake of
her frail fist out the window.

6

Nicola dreaded dinner at Thia Rita's. He loved her for what she was and tolerated the old-world figure cut by Thio Angelo. He found Aki aloof in his world of academia and Pari too brash and cocky for his liking.

The twins' fighting was boring. Angelo called the competition 'healthy', oblivious to its corrosive effect. Nicola thought it was pathetic that men in their mid-twenties still behaved like testosterone primed seventeen-year-olds.

Nicola blinked these thoughts away and concentrated on the task at hand. Thia Rita loved dark chocolate. Nicola admired the delights at Cacao Blue and settled on a selection of dark pralines. A gloved hand boxed them with the signature lime green and white ribbon.

He walked out and collided with a short elderly lady with a handcart. She lost balance before Nicola righted her and the cart, almost losing balance himself.

"Oh, you're a nice man. I was in a rush to get my tram."

Nicola gauged the accent as northern Italian. Looking at his face, her expression changed, before she rested her hand on his shoulder. Shit, she looks pale. He steered the lady to the nearest cafe and ordered her a cappuccino. As the coffee hit her system, her colour returned. She introduced herself as Stella.

"I am Stella, Stella Altezzari."

"Nicola, Nicola Petrakis."

"Ah, the rock." She formed a hard fist to make the point.

She stared into space before making eye contact again. Nicola saw the cogs turning over in her mind.

"Have we met before?" asked Nicola.

"Is your Father's name Nectario?"

"Yes, well it was. He passed away last week."

Stella opened her fist and held Nicola's hand. It was small, like a child's.

"I knew your Father Nicola. I worked at the café across from the factory. I am so sorry my child."

Nicola remembered the silly poem Nectarios used to say. Stella Bella, sweet like caramela.

He sang it out loud before stopping as Stella began crying.

"My husband passed away three years ago. Stroke. Only memories and photos are left."

"I'm sorry Stella."

"Ottavio and I shared thirty-five wonderful years together. We could not have kids, so we worked hard and travelled instead. He was my one and only. God gave and God took away."

She looked at him again and smiled.

"Nicola, your Father brightened my day. His stories, his smile. Is Lidia still with you?"

He explained Lidia's slow and gradual dementia and hoped Stella wouldn't ask to visit. She didn't. She rubbed his face.

"Those cheekbones. He was a handsome man your Father. He always spoke about taking Lidia back to Italy and Greece."

She looked at Nicola and tapped his coffee cup with her spoon to regain his attention, startling him.

"Sorry, Stella."

"Nicola, listen. You need to move on. Find her and make your own life. You are young. That is the only advice I can give you."

Despite her protests, he walked her to his car and dropped her off at her house in Fitzroy. The overhanging trees draped the street in a glorious canopy.

7

Nectarios coughed up blood in Nicola's bathroom sink to hide it from Lidia. Nicola came in to hang his towel and peered over his shoulder. Nicola forced him to see his GP.

The tests came back normal, his GP reassured him, but Nectarios remained unconvinced. At Nicola's insistence, he consulted a new doctor for the first time in thirty-five years; more tests and a biopsy Then the diagnosis; cancer in his left lung, stage 3B, inoperable. Lidia cried in private but became his rock and slept at his side through his gruelling first round of chemo. Nicola began losing concentration at work. He took leave; a week off, then a month, and then another, before taking forced leave.

One afternoon, Nectarios convinced Lidia to go home and sleep on a proper bed. She struggled to find the car. The spot was always in the same designated patient parking area. Lidia the meticulous asked a lady with a pram to help find her car. They found it as the lady drove Lidia through the car park, pushing the remote until they heard the sound.

The next morning, she left the hose on outside and flooded the garden, sending water cascading into the rear laneway. Nicola sensed something was wrong – Lidia never did that. She went into denial and focused on Nectarios while her brain lost connections. Highways in her brain closed one by one. Nectarios didn't notice the early changes at home through the fatigue of chemo, but Nicola saw them all too well; from leaving on the gas, pots of water and pasta sauce on the gas to boil dry. He waited one night until Nectarios fell asleep. He took her by the hand to the back veranda and confronted her. She didn't deny it.

"What can I do with your Father like this?"

"I'll take you to the doctor tomorrow while Dad is at the specialist. He's right around the corner."

"Your Father knows nothing. Understand?" She tapped her nose.

"Our secret." Nicola said, tapping his.

The doctor, a small man with a round face and glasses to match examined Lidia while Nicola waited outside. After three clandestine visits, a succession of blood tests, MRIs and cognitive assessments, he sat them down.

"Lidia, I'm referring you to a neurologist. We may be looking at early signs of dementia. I'm sorry."

"Me too." said Lidia.

Nicola took the referral. Three weeks later, the general consensus was stage 3 dementia: mild cognitive decline. He prepared for a long, narrow road ahead. If Nectarios found out his darling Lidia was losing her mind, it would

throttle his immune system. Nicola was certain it would
finish him off.

8

Lidia played with her penne, moving it around the plate with her fork. Mrs Calabro sat on the long bench seat opposite. The two exchanged ciao before Mr Calabro snuck up on his wife bearing gifts on each arm. A bomb went off in Lidia's brain.

An hour later, an agitated Marco dragged Nicola aside as he walked in.

"There was an episode with your Mother today."

"Narrow that down for me."

"Mrs Calabro's husband came in during lunch bearing flowers and chocolates. They started canoodling and she snapped. She threw her food at them, started abusing them. We've managed to sedate her and she's sleeping. Best we give today a miss. I've never seen her this agitated. Watching them together definitely triggered something. Maybe her subconscious is telling her something about your Father."

Nicola was sure no working notion of Nectarios existed in her conscious state but was worried what her subconscious was doing. His right temporal artery throbbed.

Lidia dreamt hard under the dense cloud of sedatives.

1968: a party in a large hall, suited up men with slicked-back hair and well-dressed women stood in hesitant groups clustered around the outside of the dancefloor. Cars drifted by, the shout of 'fucking wogs' from a HK Holden. Then came the moment her subconscious reran whenever she dreamt.

Nectarios danced with a tall Greek Aphrodite, Frank and Nancy Sinatra sang Something Stupid. The Doors' Crystal Ship started.

Before you slip into unconsciousness,
I'd like to have another kiss.

Lidia watched the couples still set up for a waltz before realising the song was four-four time. Nectarios broke away from a confused partner and locked eyes with her. Green eyes meeting her blue.

"Ciao bella. Mi chiamo Nectarios."

"Nectarios. Greco?"

"Sì."

"Lidia. Parli Italiano da tanto tempo?" Have you been speaking Italian for long?

"Sì, ma solo stasera mi serve bene. Balliamo?" Yes, but it has only been useful tonight. Shall we dance?

They now danced as Jim Morrison serenaded them.

Deliver me from reasons why,
You'd rather cry, I'd rather fly.

It was the first song she learnt in English. She smiled and
didn't wake for another four hours.

9

The short drive to Thia Rita's house didn't leave much time for reflection or centring. Nicola pulled over on a side street off Plenty Road to the annoyance of the WRX tailgating him. He tried his breathing exercises. All that came was thinking about Stella, the thought of his enraged Mother and the expected haranguing over his Father's will.

Where breathing and meditation failed, music could help. He played *Ride's* 'Leave Them All Behind'.

Wheels turning around
Into alien grounds
Pass through different times
Leave them all behind

The frenzied guitar and steadying bassline took the edge off his tension. That'll have to do he thought, as he collected his paperwork.

Rita heard the car and met him at the door before he rang the bell. She hugged him and ushered him inside.

At the table, Nicola sat to the right of his Thio Angelo, who was irritated about Rita's forays into Asian cooking.

"Nicola, help me. Is this stir fry really pork and not dog?"

"Your uncle is very old school, Nicola. Ignore him."

"How are you anyway?" Angelo asked as he delivered a blokey pat on the back.

"Day by day, Thio."

Pari and Aki walked in and greeted Nicola.

They ate, spoke about the funeral, work, everything except Lidia. Nicola resented their avoidance of his Mother since she went into the home but was grateful they didn't raise the topic here.

"Lovely meal, Thia. Thank you."

"Thank you, Nicola. I'm glad one male at the table is thankful for it."

Nicola opened a folder and removed the envelope with her cheque.

"Dad wanted me to talk to you and Sia about the will. He left both of you some money." He pushed the envelope towards her.

"And Claudio? Did he receive a cheque?"

"Dad just asked me to tell you what I told you."

Nicola donned his mental armour in anticipation. The brothers sat silent, Pari leaning forward, transfixed by the exchange to come. Angelo sat back with arms crossed. Rita looked at the cheque and placed it in her purse. She sighed and turned back to Nicola, lips pursed.

"So, if I'm correct, Claudio also got a hundred-thousand. Meaning Sia and I miss out on fifty-thousand each, even though we have kids, and he does not. Is that right?"

"Are you asking me if that is what Dad left in his will?"

"No, I am asking if it is right, if it is fair."

Missed out. Is that fair? Both temporal arteries throbbing now as he digested her words.

Unchartered waters, Nicola. Play it straight.

"That was Dad's choice, his decision. We don't have the luxury of having him here to ask him."

Angelo shook his head at Rita and raised his hand as a gesture to let it go.

"No, Angelo." Rita stared up at the ceiling and wiped her eyes. "He always said he would take care of me, your Father. And you, even if it your Father was not in a state to look after us properly, could you not see this was not enough?"

"It is not for me to decide that. It's not my will, is it? It's your brother's. And he has looked after you."

"That is your opinion," she snapped back. "All the property he had; he couldn't let one go to look after his sisters? Always greedy. No wonder he forgot to-"

Nicola collected his keys and looked at her. "I think you should leave that sentence unfinished." He bit his tongue, kissed her goodbye, her face staying put and her pout still in place, and thanked her for a lovely meal. He shook Angelo's hand and nodded at Pari.

Aki got up and walked Nicola to his car.

"I'm embarrassed and sorry, Nicola. Nothing would have been enough for her. You do what you need to do."

Aki returned and said nothing as he cleared the table. Rita and Angelo argued in their bedroom. She emerged, grabbed one of Angelo's cigarettes and lit up outside, slamming the door hard, almost lifting the slider off its hinges.

Where would you like to store this, Nicola? He asked himself this question out loud as he started down the road. Visit Sia now and be done with it. It was a six-song drive. *Blur's* '1992' was ending as he slowed to park outside her house in Thornbury. Guitar distortions, piano and Damon Albarn's anguished high pitched cries dissolved into silence.

Nicola shut the engine. He jumped as Petra tapped on his window.

Nicola braced himself for another confrontation. The hallway opened up into a large open plan living/kitchen area. Sia hugged him and smiled.

"Just got off the phone with my sister."

Nicola let her continue.

"Nicola, you are my brother's messenger. I am not upset with you. This is how it is. Unlike Rita, I know how it feels to have lost someone from my life. It fucking hurts. When Achilles died, Petra was only twelve. I only thank God he arranged things. We're not struggling, and neither is the wicked witch of the north, don't worry. You still have Lidia, poor Lidia to look after as well as yourself. Your Father raised me, and I never thanked him enough. Rita forgets history when it is convenient for her."

Nicola handed Sia her cheque and watched Petra ogle at the numbers. He could almost hear her counting the five zeros.

Despite an excellent coffee and some brownies, Nicola began nodding off. He needed little convincing to stay over. He refused the spare bed and fell asleep on the couch. As Nicola's preferred babysitter, Sia was used to tucking him in.

In her bedroom, Petra lay on her side. She was unable to think of anything else but her encounter of a week ago.

Petra knocked on Professor Kondos' open door. He called her in and waved her to a seat with a smile as he spoke on the phone. Petra estimated him at five-foot eleven, but his shaven head and muscular form made him intimidating to many of his students. No one dared talk during his lectures.

Kondos ended his call and looked at Petra. "What's up?"

"Professor Kondos, I'm unprepared for the final anatomy exam next week."

"Are there any personal circumstances I should know about?"

"My dearest uncle died of cancer. The funeral is the day after the exam."

"I'm sorry for your loss. How are you and your family coping?"

"We're getting there. Is there scope for-"

"Special consideration? That's up to my discretion." A lengthy pause.

He stood and faced the bookshelf behind his desk and rearranged books and folders before turning to Petra with a manila folder in his hand.

"OK, let's have a look, shall we?"

He brought up her file on the screen and referred from it to the folder. He sat back and rested his feet on the desk, looking in silence between his screen and an imaginary space on the desk between them. Petra picked at her thumbnail, tried to stop and picked again as Kondos weighed up her fate. A pain shot up through her lower abdomen. Her periods had been violently painful lately and she struggled not to squirm. He finally made eye contact.

"You are passing your core subjects," he said with a faint smile. "But without a pass in Anatomy, and I remind you that this Anatomy exam is a hurdle exam, you risk repeating the year. All subjects." Special emphasis on hurdle and all.

He let that sit and stared at the space above Petra's head, before lowering his gaze.

He stood up and walked to her side of the table. "Or perhaps we can help each other?"

"We all experience grief and stress," his tone went higher. He rubbed her shoulder then ran his hand up her neck and through her hair.

"Can we help each other Petra?"

Petra's heart raced as Kondos made eye contact again. He used her indecision and shock to press his lips into her mouth, before he pushed then bent her over his table, one hand forcing her pants down, the other firm between

her shoulder blades, thumb and index finger tight against
the base of her neck. She froze for what seemed forever
before she re-engaged with the present. He was moving
inside her and the friction sent a hot pain through her. As
soon as Kondos eased pressure on her back, she
summoned all her energy and twisted away, kicking in
the same motion. She caught Kondos in the balls and sent
him to the floor groaning in pain. Pants pulled up, she ran
down the corridor and willed the lift to arrive, listening in
panic for any footsteps. She ran to her car and cried, then
drove home and cried in the shower as the pain returned.

Kondos nursed his unexpected embarrassment. He
relived the encounter later and came in the shower.

 Petra took a morning-after pill, a Naproxen and
showered three times a day in the days that followed. She
found it difficult to open a textbook, and her skin itched
as the rape played in her head. Sia didn't find it unusual
that Petra was quiet and took her dinner in her room; she
did it during year twelve exams and put it down to exam
stress and her period. Petra found pretending to her
Mother exhausting. When it became too much, she rang a
university counselling service, before hanging up when
the warm, maternal voice asked how she could help.

Petra accepted she needed to be pragmatic and get
through this exam. She expected her emotions would
ambush her once the wall of exams was over. Having to
repeat second year, having to sit through Kondos
lecturing motivated her. She exercised to near exhaustion
and pictured Kondos' face with every punch at the gym.

After a few false starts, she found a study system that worked. She attached all the possible questions she thought likely to be asked onto her bedroom wall in her own writing. She answered them verbally, walking from question to question and back again. She banked on the circle of Willis and renal structure as being certainties to be included in the exam and spent time perfecting her answers to both. Hearing her own voice empowered her and minimised distractions. On the day of the exam, she expected Kondos to be there and was relieved he wasn't. She left the three-hour exam early, confident she did well enough to pass. She slept and prepped for her last two exams in pathology and microbiology.

After her last exam, a calm came over Petra. She waited for depression to fill the void left by the end exams and braced herself, but instead was filled with a burning desire for Kondos to suffer.

She considered telling Nicola. He was piled up with grief and responsibility, but on the other hand, there was no one else she could tell.

Nicola made coffee in the morning and left a short note for Sia and Petra. At around six, he drove home and showered. He was relieved that Sia bore no grudges about the will.

As the bank's first customer, he presented his letter, ID and key for Dad's safety box. He the box and began with a letter. Nicola recognised his Father's clear cursive, a trait Nectarios took immense pride in.

Nicola,

While I can still think and write, I need to tell you a few things.

Please be with your Mother when you can. You have a life to live but your Mother is your Mother. Where she stopped recognizing me, she remembers you. I have been at peace with that for some time, even if it hurts. You and Claudio are the only people she knows. Whatever life she has will need you in it.

I am sure the will has caused some distress among my sisters. Rita got upset because I gave money to Claudio for sure. Nothing was ever enough for her, even as a teenager and after she got married. My baby sister Sia. She understood. Am I right?

Nicola smiled.

> *Your Mother and I made you old before your time. I am sorry, but nature is nature and you are tough enough to face it.*
>
> *I hope I passed on more than money and genes to you. When I married outside the Greek community, I was an outsider. Now it happens every day. It is normal. No one has a special pedigree. We are all animals, mixed in this zoo called life as we pretend that we are better than the animals that walk on four legs. They say Fathers should be Fathers to their sons and not friends, but I found it impossible not to be your friend too. I will miss our peripato of the mind.*
>
> *I hope you remembered to put some of Lidia's hair in my hands before they closed me up as I asked you.*
>
> *Find someone to spend your life with. Find Gigi, find out why. Maybe all is not lost.*
>
> *Your Father, Nectarios.*

Nicola welled up. He took his time placing items in his backpack: a worn leather wallet, mixed keys, documents and photos. He completed the formalities and handed back the safety box. He was at Claudio's house twenty minutes later. He gave him his cheque and they left.

As they drove to Santa Croce, Nicola recounted the edited version of the confrontation with Mrs Calabro.

"Did they say something to her?"
"No, just a bad day to go with the good days. And worse ones."

"Natura brutta." Ugly nature.

Lidia was watching Kingswood Country when they walked in, wagging her finger at Ted calling Bruno a wog.

"Stu' Bastardo Ted."

"No swearing Mum."

"Let's go out to the garden," she said.

Claudio held her arm and supported her as she got up.

Lidia's eyes squinted as the sunlight hit them, then adapted and opened wide as she tried to absorb as much warmth and light as possible.

"Che bel sole!"

They sat on a thick, low lying branch of an enormous oak tree that ran parallel to the ground. It was carved, sanded and polished with great care by Marco's Father to make a smooth seat.

Lidia was content sitting on the seat until clouds came.
She began to shiver.

"Madonna, che freddo."
Claudio and Nicola helped her up to her room and sat
with her, rugging her up till she drifted off.

11

Nicola broke routine the next day. He took the 96 tram down Nicholson, got off at Collins St and walked the fifty metres uphill.

Stefan Zivkovic was easy to spot from his enormous bald head and the eagle tattoo on the back of his broad neck. Colleagues at Victoria Police wondered if it signified right-wing sympathies. Zivkovic liked keeping people guessing despite having no such leanings. His large hand squeezed Nicola's and held for an uncomfortable few seconds.

"Nicola, my condolences. I lost my Dad three years ago. It gets easier."

"Thanks, Stefan. Does your offer still hold?"

"Always. We plan your re-entry and kick it upstairs to make sure it gets an OK. You've got me to vouch for you. You could do with a steppingstone though. You left with good reason, no qualms there. But dropping back in right after your Father passing and with your Mother still under care will raise eyebrows. Maybe counselling would be good to ease you back in?"

"I need counselling?"

"No, I meant you doing some counselling. Bread and butter stuff. I'm not asking by the way, I'm telling you. If you're in a stable psychological state and flexing your analytical muscles again, it'll make it much easier to draft you back in."

"Ok. Give me time to organise something."

"Take all the time you need. Look for an inner suburban GP. Lots of elderly wogs, hipsters and trans-whatevers with issues. You'll be like Motherfucking Teresa to them. Stay in touch."

A last sip and a slap on the back, and Zivkovic was gone.

Nicola thought it through. During his Clinical Psychology Masters, he developed an algorithm for assessing vocational suitability. He further tweaked it to measure applicant suitability for new roles and internal promotions. From a commercial standpoint, this became desirable. It landed him a role at Biopsych, a company that did psychometric testing for companies hiring new staff. As the owner of the intellectual property, he insisted on doing the processing himself. When Biopsych asked to buy the algorithm, he negotiated a healthy sale price and a three-year contract in the deal. Nicola couldn't pinpoint when he became bored, but the feeling stayed with him and in his third year, he decided to leave.

When Victoria Police doubled its forensic psychology department, Nicola became interested. It was far more interesting than the vanilla work at Biopsych.

12

Lidia ate breakfast, got dressed and let herself out. It was that simple. A dramatic family meeting entangled Marco. The nurse that did not call in sick went to the toilet and gave Lidia the time she needed. She giggled like a little girl at the ease of her escape. She walked the hundred metres to Burgundy Street and hailed a taxi.

"Carlton Cemetery please." she said, producing a fifty dollar note from her bag.

13

At just after ten a.m., Nicola received the call from Marco. He rang Claudio on the way and met him there. A thorough search of the grounds and rooms yielded nothing. Nicola sat as Claudio paced.

"How can you sit Nicola?"

"I'm thinking."

Lidia, so keen to go outside. Maybe she wanted to take it one step beyond the tree seat. Where would she go? Nicola ran to his car and hoped he was right.

"Wait here in case she returns." he yelled as he left.

Claudio scratched his head.

Nicola parked near the MacPherson Street entrance and walked straight to Nectarios. Nope, fuck. Running, running with no strategy. Nicola looked for Lidia among the widows in black checking in on their husbands. He then turned at the sound of her voice. A woman in sunglasses and a blue dress with a floral pattern led Lidia to a seat.

"Thank you so much." said Nicola to the woman.

"That's Ok. Your Mother seems disoriented."

"Thank you so much. Mum, what are you doing?"

"Aurelia. Where is she?"

"Aurelia isn't here. Cremated."

"Cremata? Pagani."

Nicola turned to thank the woman again, but she had already reached the gate. He raised his hand in obligation to say thanks. Lidia crossed her arms the whole trip back to Heidelberg, only uncrossing them to express her disgust.

"Cremating people is wrong. Would you cremate your Mother?" she asked a man two graves away.

"We are Serbian. We bury our people with dignity," replied the man, with the emphasis on dignity.

"You see?"

When Lidia got angry, she often broke into English. Nicola made the mistake he always made and responded in Italian, thinking it would calm her.

"Propria lei voleva cosi." That's what she wanted.

"I don't care. It's WRONG!" she replied and looked out the window until they arrived.

Marco's remaining hair was pointing out at all angles as Nicola walked Lidia back in. He oversaw Lidia's resettlement, then took Nicola and Claudio back to his office.

"Nicola, I apologise for this."

"She's OK now. I really don't want to do this, but can we move my Mother to a more secure area, so this doesn't happen again?"

"We can. It's your call."

"Ok, let's do it."

Claudio's face looked anguished before he feebly nodded. Nausea kicked in at the thought of imprisoning his Mother. He barely made it to the bathroom when he got home and threw up. He showered and rested in front of the TV. He found *The Sopranos* and watched until two in the morning. Livia was resentful about being shoved into Greengrove and manipulating all and sundry; Tony, Uncle Junior, everyone. He wiped the comparison from his mind and went to sleep.

Dr Robert Collina looked at Claudio. He looked down and slumped.

"How's Lidia?"

"She's caged."

"What do you mean?"

She took a taxi to Carlton Cemetery and left us no choice but to go into tighter security."

"How are you, Claudio?"

"How do you think I am? I am the last healthy member of my family. My sister is dying in instalments. Me, the healthy one, what a waste."

"How so?"

"God sent me an angel, gave her cancer and took her away. All that is left is death to look forward to. Lidia should be healthy, not me. Without Morena I am nothing."

"That is very pessimistic Claudio. Every person should afford themselves some kindness. You can't survive thinking like this." He paused. "What about a holiday?"

"Italy? There is no one there. Both of my parents were only children. The last. Australia is beautiful enough, thank you."

"Ok, good. You love fishing. You say it calms you. Get away for a week."

"Then I have to come back."

"We all do Claudio. But what if you came back feeling better? Small wins are good."

"This medication, how long should it take to work? "

"Lexapro takes two or three weeks. I prescribed it a month ago. Let's bump up the dose a little bit."

Claudio looked at the script. His eyes ached as he remembered ridiculing anyone needing tablets for depression. Depression is a weakness, he used to say.

15

Nicola jumped at the chance to go fishing when Claudio rang him that night. He found three of Nectarios' favourite rods. All were well maintained with reels that spun like a dream.

Claudio pulled up at four a.m. They made a solitary stop at Lakes Entrance for coffee, homemade panini and a driver change. By mid-afternoon, they were fishing off Tathra Wharf. Nicola tried lures while Claudio stuck with pilchards and prawns on the other side. Nicola lost an impressive Spanish mackerel halfway between water and rod as the marvellous specimen broke the line, twisting free in mid-air and splashing back to safety. Laughter and pity came from fellow anglers. Claudio bagged a brace of tailor. Nicola redeemed himself with a dozen flathead after changing to bait. They fished on into an hour of darkness.

Claudio rested his rod and rubbed his wrist.

"Arthritis playing up?"

"Uffa the bastard. It gets me when I fish."

"I loved it when you and Dad used to drive me up here."

"You used to sleep the whole way. Tomorrow we'll try Bournda Beach early for salmon."

Nicola was the closest thing to a son Claudio would ever
have, yet he had no concept of what having his own child
would be like. This cut him off from friends with
children and who went away with other families with
children. Claudio's circle included his sister, Nectarios
and Nicola for company, but not in the presence of Rita.
Her hatred became obvious soon after Lidia married
Nectarios. Claudio and Nectarios shared a mutual
respect, enforced on the day before their wedding when
Lidia demanded that they get on like brothers. She
wouldn't tolerate anything less. Their friendship grew
year by year and they became close.

Nicola nodded off in seconds. Claudio tossed and turned
for an hour. He put it down to the increased Lexapro.
After two trips to the toilet, he finally found sleep.

Petra sat in her final tutorial for the year, in her own world and nodding at whatever was said. She still wondered whether she could tell Nicola, let alone the Police or the University about Associate Professor Kondos. Kondos, the respected authority with a wall decorated by awards, degrees and fellowships, and at forty-five, into his fourth year as Head of the Anatomy Department. Petra doubted anyone would believe her.

She decided to confide in Nicola. She could only rerun those five minutes so many times. The girl next to her gave her a nudge, pointing out the irritated glare of the prac leader. She asked her twice in a flat, tired voice to describe the nerves that form the pulmonary plexus and was about to ask a third time. She redeemed herself without missing a beat.

"Parasympathetic nerves from the vagus nerve and sympathetic nerves from the upper thoracic and cervical ganglia of the sympathetic trunk."

Deprived of her chance to embarrass her, the tutor nodded. A few minutes later, her phone vibrated - notification from the faculty that she had passed the year. No exam results, these would come later. She cried in a toilet as she read the message again before walking to her car, the sunshine warm and welcoming. She looked forward to the break.

Nicola arrived home just before midnight. He put the filleted fish in the garage freezer, stored the fishing gear away and took a much-needed shower. They had gone to town on the salmon off Bournda beach and he reeked of it.

The next morning, he read the text from Petra.

Free for a coffee today?
        Sure. Brunetti's @ 12 ok?
Done. c u then. P x

Nicola enjoyed the warmth as he walked to the cemetery. He turned the corner and noticed a woman stopping at Nectarios' plot. He walked the long way around and watched her while pretending to tend to another grave. She bent down over his photo and passed a kiss from her mouth to Nectarios' photo, the hand lingering for a second. She then placed a fresh bunch of flowers in a vase, arranging them around the ones still alive while discarding the dead ones. She's good with her hands. A surgeon? Many doctors saw Nectarios during his journey, but he didn't remember this one. Why would a doctor pass a kiss? And linger? And then she was gone. Nicola caught himself tiptoeing to his Dad's plot in case she caught him. The arranged flowers showed good taste. There was no indent from heels. He added practicality to the list.

"Was she nice Dad? Where do you know her from? I took your rods fishing with Claudio in Narooma. We caught some salmon, flatties and tailor. Mum's Ok. She may have passed by here recently. She snuck out for a little visit, you remember how clever she can be. She's safe again."

He sat for a further ten minutes before catching a tram to Brunetti.

Petra had the back section to herself with the breakfast surge gone and the lunch rush an hour away. She had already smashed a strong latte. He hugged her and took one look at her.

"You Ok, Petra?"

"I will be."

"What's going on?"

"Look I shouldn't tell you. You're still grieving but-"

"I'm OK, just tell me."

She mentally rearranged what she was going to say, aware of Nicola's impatience. "Don't edit," he said.

She leaned in. "My anatomy professor raped me."

Her voice shook as she strained to whisper the words. Her pupils dilated and facial muscles tightened. Nicola

held her hands, Petra squeezed back in return as she
started crying.

"What, when?"

"Four days before the funeral."

"Are you OK?"

"I'm...better. Please, let me get it out because..."

Nicola set himself as Petra tried to verbalise what had
been replaying in her head. He was patient as she told
him what had happened.

"I ran to my car and drove home to wash clean. I
couldn't wash it all off, like I was dirty."

"No, no, no. He preyed on your indecision. He used his
power and that is all rape is about. Power. Whether you
passed or failed meant nothing to him. He took it out of
your hands."

"What am I supposed to do now?"

"Did you take the exam?" *You idiot, what a question,*
thought Nicola.

"Yes, some of the questions I banked on turned up and I
passed. What are you thinking Nicola?"

"Have you spoken to anyone about it? Police, university?"

"No, only you." She cried and found it too hard to stop. Nicola cradled her head against his chest while thoughts of vengeance raced through his head.

"I'm here for you, but you need some counselling, as in someone besides me. I can recommend someone for you."

"I'm happy enough that we've spoken to you about it."

"You may need another woman to speak to. I can recommend someone for you."

He gave her the name of a colleague who worked in crisis centres.

"Please. Make a time."

"Ok, I will. But how many others have there been? It was like I was mute from fright until it happened."

"Petra this was not his first time. What's his name?"

"Savvas Kondos."

Nicola kept eye contact as he heard the name. He remembered taking a neuroanatomy unit with him, twelve weeks in all. He was eager to help the female students while playing the alpha male, skewering any male student who made the slightest mistake.

"You recognise the name, don't you?"

"It rings a bell."

"What are you thinking Nicola?"

"I think we should call the police."

"Because my word will hold up against his? You said it yourself, it's power. The other girls he's done this to have either been given passes, dropped out or were too scared. Either way, it can't be proven."

"Let me think about it."

As he walked her to her car, he weighed up in his mind about how to inflict damage on this monster. He knew full well that he was as much indulging himself as he was countenancing revenge out of solidarity for his cousin. He looked forward to confronting the bastard.

Petra smiled and looked forward to the study break.

18

Dr Alex Kapadis sipped her coffee in the staff room after her last rush of patients. She poured over her letters, mostly invitations from Pharmaceutical companies which she threw into recycling. She wondered why she bothered cooking when she could eat out on the account of Pfizer, Pharma, GSK and others. She looked up as Dr Carlo di Panzaro walked in waving a giant Collingwood fan hand.

"You're nothing but a big kid Carlo. Isn't the footy season over?"

"It's Collingwood Fan Day tomorrow. Wanna come?"

"I hate Collingwood. Hate footy even more."

"Snob."

"Yob."

"So, what does a hot single Greek doctor do on a Friday night?"

"I avoid men in the city who think they are hot. I rest and enjoy my own company or that of my friends. To that end, there is a five-kilometre idiot radius from the GPO that I avoid."

She called her Mother and told her she'd be home in
twenty minutes.

Lidia walked to her bathroom. She washed her hands and looked in the mirror. The man with dark brown hair and green eyes stood behind her, an expectant expression on his face. His edges were hazy, like a ghost of love returned, but his smell was so real to her that she opened her nostrils wide, inhaling until she thought her lungs would burst. His arms were now around her waist and his smooth shaved face kissed her left ear. And like that he was gone. Lidia shuffled back to bed and willed time to pass until he came back.

After a late Saturday breakfast, Nicola estimated it to be a pleasant twenty degrees. He walked to visit Nectarios. He stayed for a few minutes and saw the flowers askew. Maybe she's gone. He began walking into Carlton to check out Readings. Walking down Cardigan St, he stopped and patted himself down to realise he had dropped his phone. He raced back to find it next to the plot and dusted it off.

Crossing Lygon St was the woman with the good hands. He realised as she got closer that she was the same woman who found walkabout Lidia. He dashed behind some trees and waited. She bent over the photo and gave the same kiss to Nectarios. Who is this woman? He shuddered at the thought of Nectarios with a woman this young. She wore a dark blue dress and ankle high black leather boots. Nicola estimated her to be in her late twenties.

For the first time, Nicola took notice of her in isolation, not who she was to his Father or how she found Lidia, though that question still needed an answer. He broke into a sweat and choked back a sudden urge to throw up. A tingling travelled down the right side of his lower back. The tingling got stronger as the woman got up without warning and strode towards him.

"You!" she yelled, pointing her finger. "Don't move."

How can I? thought Nicola, his legs feeling rooted deep into the earth.

Alex Kapadis shortened the distance in quick time. She stood with hands on hips, eyeballing her voyeur.

"Who the hell are you?" Nicola got in first.

"You first." Alex boomed back.

"I'm Nicola, Nectarios' son. Nectarios of the grave you've been visiting, curating and giving kisses. Care to explain?"

Alex grabbed Nicola in a hug and said, "I'm so sorry for your loss."

Her hug was too strong for a woman of her size. Nicola was nauseous again and had to free himself. He leaned on the nearest tree for support and dry retched. He asked her again, noticing her green eyes and straight dark brown hair. She had her head tilted at a slight angle he recognised. No, no, no he said to himself.

"Who are you? You find my Mother and then twice visit my Father's grave. Bit more than a coincidence, no?"

"This will take a few coffees. I'm Alex." she said and surprised him with a kiss on the cheek. She grabbed his hand and led him to her car. Nicola felt so weak he could have been led by a five-year old. Alex moved her bag from the passenger seat and ushered him in. She drove the short distance to Rathdowne St and got a park right in front of the Paragon.

"Nice Dermie." said Nicola.

"Nice what?"

"Dermie. It's a euphemism. As in Dermott Brereton, you know, the football player. He's renowned for getting the best spots wherever he goes."

"No. I don't know. What is it with you guys and bloody football?"

Coffees ordered; Nicola scrutinised her. Explain yourself. A woman who drank short blacks would an upfront type. He chided himself for using coffee pop psychology. The hands on the clock opposite was blurry and he struggled to make out the time.

"Well?" he asked.

"Your Dad and I. Scratch that. Your Dad. Your Dad- he had a fling with my Mum, Rena. They ended it, well, my Mother ended it because she felt bad for your Mother. And here I am."

"Here you are what?"

"She became pregnant and decided to keep me. I'm your half-sister."

"Bullshit." came the reflex response.

Alex placed her hand over Nicola's and felt the clenched hardness. Nectarios had a grip and strength that belied his modest physique. He felt nauseous again.

"That's Ok. I expected that knee jerk response. Look, Mum is still alive. Care to meet her? She couldn't come to the funeral, not after all these years of never seeing him again and only reading about it in *Neos Kosmos*. Imagine her shock. She asked me to visit the grave, give him a kiss and bring flowers for her."

"How old is your Mother?"

"Sixty-two."

"And you?"

"Thirty-six. You?"

"Thirty-four. What do you do?" As he asked the question, he did the maths. Mum and Dad were married two and a half years when they had me.

"I'm a GP."

"The way you handled the flowers the other day I had you pegged as a surgeon. I'm a psychologist."

Nicola's pulse dropped to a comfortable level and the strobing had stopped. He smiled for the first time since the stand-off. Alex smiled back.

"Look, I've known of you for a while. Mum never told me about Nectarios until I was 18. She told me that my Father died when I was three from a stroke. Took me years to forgive her. But I understood her point of view. It was always only the two of us anyway."

"Were you ever tempted to see him, Nectarios?"

"Of course I was. But Mum made me promise not to. It took a lot for her to end it with him. She was very strong and didn't want your Mother finding out. I had no intention of betraying her."

"That's very noble of you."

They sat, both reconciling the new information and assessing new family, the new background of their existence. Nicola presumed the fling happened after his parents were married. Alex studied his face for a reaction.

"How did you find my Mother the other day?" asked Nicola.

'Pure luck, honestly. I didn't even know it was your Mother till I saw you. She was wandering from headstone to headstone looking for an Aurelia. She was cold and I was about to escort her back to my car to take her to her home when you arrived. I was going to be late for my shift and left."

"Convenient."

"Thanks is the word you're after Nicola. This is a shock for me too, you know, meeting my half-brother for the first time. Did you think I was going to stick around and shoot the breeze with you under the circumstances?"

"Sorry and thank you."

"And before you ask, Mum and I aren't after any money or property. He looked after Mum. He was a decent man to her."

"That hadn't entered my mind Alex. I believe you. Those eyes and the way you tilt your head are pure Nectarios. I don't need a DNA test."

More silence.

"How advanced is your Mum's dementia?"

"She is still classed grade 3, mild cognitive decline. She stopped recognising Dad for the last six months of his life. She only recognises me and her brother, Claudio. She is at risk of stroke, has a cluster A personality disorder which makes her a charmer for the fellow residents. After that day she went walkabout, we had to move her to a more secure area. Apart from that, she's fine."

Alex cupped his elbow and rubbed his forearm with her thumb.

"I'm sorry to hear it. And Dad, I mean Nectarios. What cancer was it?"

"You can call him Dad. Lung. He fought it hard and was stable before it spread to his bones, lungs, brain."

Nicola's brain filled with a surge of questions.

"Where do you and Rena live?"

"Northcote."

"I would like to meet her one day."

Alex's phone blipped. "Shit, gotta go but can we catch up again in a couple of days? I'll contact you."

They exchanged numbers. Nicola watched her drive away and sang to himself.

Nobody told me there'd be days like these,
Nobody told me there'd be days like these,
Strange days indeed,
Most peculiar Mama.

21

Nicola caught himself fidgeting as he sat waiting. His childhood friend's voice reassured a woman she didn't need to come in weekly. Her face suggested the need was far from therapeutic. Dr Leonidas Kaspar turned to him and smiled, his muscular frame masked well by his white coat, a throwback to more traditional times he refused to let go of.

"Do you have time for me, Dr K?"

"Nicola, well this is a surprise. Come in, buddy. I would have met you halfway you know."

"Melton isn't far, Leo. How's dermatology?"

Leonidas shrugged. "It's OK. I'm not good for much else." He assessed Nicola as he sat. "Did they accept your passport? It isn't close to much. How are you coping? I hardly saw you at the funeral. I didn't want to bother you."

"It's funny. None on the friendships I made during Uni have lasted yet you've been there from the first day we went to kinder together."

"I'm honoured, Nicola. But how are you going?"

"I'm Ok. Actually, I lie. My grieving has been interrupted."

"Sorry?"

"I'm angry at him."

"Nectarios?"

"Yes."

Leonidas motioned him to go on with his hands.

"A few months after he married my Mother, he had an affair with a woman and got her pregnant. The daughter showed up at Dad's grave yesterday. I have a half-sister now."

"And she wants money?"

"No, she's self-sufficient, a GP. Lives with her Mother."

"So why are you angry?"

Nicola tapped his fingers as he made his points. "Because he didn't tell me, didn't tell me there was someone else, that he cheated on my Mother, that I might have to deal with this after he was gone; he just left, left it for me to deal with. I can't tell Mum with her dementia. Dad's gone, so all I can do is shout at his grave."

"Have you said that out loud before?"

"No."

"Now that you have, do you feel better?"

"To be honest, I don't know."

"And that's Ok too. Just don't bury your anger, it only comes back louder."

"I'm sorry for coming here after not seeing you for over a year."

"Again with that? I went through this three years ago, remember? You were there at all hours of the day for me. You call me in five minutes or five years, I'm still the same person - your friend, Ok?"

"Thanks. How's Isabel?"

"We split about four months ago. We're Ok with it. Michael lives with me. He's twelve now- amazing little bloke. Wants to do psychiatry. Other kids are up to their necks in Harry Potter and gaming, and his bedroom is full of Jung and Freud."

"I'm sorry to hear that, Leon."

"Which part?" They laughed at the joke before the buzzer rang. Kaspar excused himself with a quick hug.

"Anytime, OK? I'll come to you and revisit civilisation sometime."

Nicola's mood improved on the drive home. He walked
back to the cemetery, sat on the grass and looked at his
Father's picture.

"Why, Dad? Wasn't Mum enough? You let me find out
like this? Now you give me a sibling?"

After the third miscarriage, Nectarios urged Lidia not to
give up. Her doctor told her it would be risky to keep
trying, but Nectarios dismissed the advice and took Lidia
away to Eden for a week. He waited on her every need
and by the third day, she was ready to try again. A year
ago, Rena had given birth to a girl, so he knew he was
fertile, and his guilt fuelled him to do whatever it took to
have a child with Lidia. She called the girl Alex. The
thought of not being able to see and raise his only child
drove him mad. When Lidia fell pregnant and moved
past four months, he cried with relief. Nicola made them
wait though, choosing to come into the world five days
after the due date, causing Lidia gestational diabetes and
a faltering liver. Nectarios begged to try again when
Nicola was a year old. He needed a girl of his own to
hold but Lidia put her foot down. Her mind and body
were not up to another try. Nectarios sent Alex a gift
every year until Rena came to his work and asked him
discreetly to stop, her irritation clear.

Nicola sat a while longer. He tried to see things from his
parents' perspective. He wondered if his parents had
issues conceiving and whether he himself was a miracle.
Lidia's parents were only children themselves, and he
speculated that maybe they tried for another child after

her but couldn't manage. He had no idea and could ask no one, but soon the anger lifted. He walked home and played 'Let Forever Be' by *The Chemical Brothers* on repeat. He drew a line under the angst and decided to move on.

22

The vibration woke Nicola just after seven a.m. He blinked twice to clear his eyes as he read the message on his phone.

You're coming to dinner tonight. See you at 730. Bring nothing.
51 Salford St Northcote.
x Alex

His finger hovered over the screen before he left it unanswered.

After he showered his phone beeped again.

I know you've read my text Nicola. Call me so we can end this weirdness.

She answered on the first ring.

"Morning, Nicola, Are we OK?"

"Are you always this efficient?"

"Yes. Are you coming tonight?"

"I'm still messed up over this. Dinner this soon is a bit much at the moment."

"You're meeting my Mother. Did you want to Skype her first to break the ice? You shouldn't have said you wanted to meet her if you didn't mean it."

"I'm sorry."

"I can see how you're upset at your Father for not telling you. But you're not the only one here, Nicola. I'm also alone in this world, and you're not depriving me of the only sibling I will ever have, so you can add pain in the arse to efficient. My Mother is a little lamb. You have nothing to fear from her. Promise me you'll come. For your sister?"

He surveyed the family pictures on the lounge wall, the sole child in every image.

"I'm bringing dessert."

He drove off to get coffee on the way to see his Mother. Claudio got in and grunted good morning. Nicola knew the face and let him be. Before they got out of the car, Claudio squeezed Nicola's arm.

"Promise me one thing OK?" said Claudio.

"Anything."

"If I get where your Mother is, you turn the machine off. I want you to fix the paper, so you are my powerful attorney. I don't want to suffer like her."

"You mean power of attorney."

"Nicola, don't make fun of me."

"I'm not. What brought this on?"

Claudio stared into the distance. "For me, there is nothing left."

"You are fit and healthy. You can control over whatever you want to do. Your sister cannot. Aren't you being a little dramatic?"

"Dramatic? No, Nicola. God took my chance at happiness away."

"Since then nothing else happened because you closed your mind to the possibility of meeting someone else."

"Nicola, all respect, you are a bit young to say this. When your destiny, your reason for living is taken away," Claudio made a blowing motion over his palm like a child blowing the white puffs of a dandelion, "the reason to live is gone. I should be in that bed, not your Mother. Nature made a big mistake here."

"Nature doesn't always get it right." said Nicola.

Nicola rubbed his back. Claudio asked Nicola to wait while he composed himself. They walked in as Lidia combed her hair. Her lipstick was on the bedside table.

For the first time in years, her make up box was open, its mirror reflecting.

He ushered Claudio towards Lidia and whispered to Pina, a waif-like woman who Lidia gravitated to.

"How long has this been happening?"

"This? Four, five days. She gets herself dolled up and sits up doing her hair, makeup. She goes to her bathroom and stays for ten, fifteen minutes, sometimes longer. Then she comes out and takes her makeup off again. She smiles like she's been on a date. I know that face."

"How often?"

Pina looked up at Nicola's eyes and added, "once a day, sometimes twice."

They sat with Lidia for half an hour. No one dared to knock her off her cloud. Nicola knew Nectarios was active in Lidia's subconscious, a new yet familiar figure in her life worth getting made up for. Best she saw him like this.

23

Nicola dropped Claudio home and found a park on Grattan St. He found a cafe and made a call to Victoria Police. Kondos' details and background were easy enough to gather, especially when the person providing them was a former colleague and friend. He thanked her and looked at the scribbles on the page in front of him, creating a mental amalgam of its separate components. He finished his coffee and walked across to a bench in a quiet spot on the North Lawn of Melbourne University. It was overcast and the grass was lush and soft. He filtered out the noise and rang Kondos' number. He wanted to hear his voice and listen for the tone. Kondos answered on the second ring.

"Professor Kondos."

"Professor Kondos, how long has it been your practice to offer female students in exam limbo a *quid pro quo*?"

"Excuse me?"

"A *quid pro quo*. Something for something."

"I understand Latin. I'm an anatomy professor."

"Ok then, sex for grades."

"Who is this?" There it was, the slight upward inflection.

"Actually, let's drop the niceties and up it straight to rape. How would Olivia react if she knew you were a rapist, Professor?"

Nicola's pulse quickened at the sound of curtains being pulled and a door being shut.

"So, I now have your attention. I'm not calling you from outside your building. I wonder though, your little girls, Maya and Grace; they'll be the same age one day as the girls you have raped. But right now, my concern is what you did to my daughter." Click.

Kondos redialled the number. Nicola let it ring six times before answering.

"Yes?" Said Nicola.

"Do you have any idea what you're fucking accusing me of?"

"No doubt in my mind. And before you rattle off your accreditations and impress me with your academic standing, some reality. It means nothing, fuck all. If what my daughter said didn't happen, then why call back in such a panic? Hand yourself in or let circumstances deal you what you get."

"Are you threatening me?"

"Not personally, but karma can be tortuous, like say the splenic artery or that weed that manages to break through cracks in concrete. You wonder how it made it that far, but it finds a way. Hand yourself in. Last chance.”

He waited and heard silence but for a sharp intake of breath.

“Look, I’d love to chat, but this is a prepaid and my credit’s almost out.”

He hung on the line a further six seconds and hung up. When Kondos called back, he let it ring out.

Nicola played back the call in his head and was satisfied. He reviewed the background information on Kondos; married to Olivia, thirty-seven, a GP with two young girls; Maya, eight and Grace, six. His ascension into the role of Head of Anatomy was quicker than anyone expected. Kondos cultivated a high level of respect in the academic community.

Nicola turned to the gift for Rena and Alex. How do you choose a gift for a woman who your Father cheated on your Mother with? Five minutes late, he waited for *The Horrors’* Sea Within A Sea to finish. He enjoyed the silence at the end of the song, the ethereal tones pulsing and resonating for a few seconds until actual silence replaced it. He collected the yellow irises and ricotta cannoli off the passenger seat and knocked on the door. Alex pulled him through the door and said *be nice* before introducing him to Rena. Rena kissed him and ran her eyes over his face as she held his forearms.

"Those green eyes I recognise."

"Yes, green. My Mothers are blu-"

He tried to catch his words. Alex rolled her eyes as Rena led the way into the living area.

Rena answered the oven's shrill tone and took the roast lamb out to rest. The smell of rosemary, oregano, garlic and lemon swept through the small house. He looked at the photos around the room. A small faded black and white photo of a young Rena and Nectarios caught his eye.

"Nosy, aren't we?" whispered Alex.

"Wouldn't you be? Sorry, but you can't blame me for being curious."

"Be curious without being curious. She's shaking as it is."

"Look at the grip marks on my arms. She's is fine shape if you ask me.'"

"Be a good guest."

"I will."

"I saved my best lamb for you, Nicola," proclaimed Rena. Roast lamb, potatoes and a salad of rocket, beetroot and goat's cheese with pine nuts kept the trio

busy. Rena plucked up the courage, sucking in deep
breaths before speaking.

"Your Father held his hands the same way you do while
he chewed, dipped his bread in the gravy just like you.
He always poured me a drink without asking like you do.
He was a lovely man, Nicola. Forgive me for saying this,
but I loved your Father."

"It's Ok, Rena. You don't need to ask forgiveness."

"I am sure you are just a little bit angry to find out?"

"I have dealt with it, Rena. I am not angry at all with
you."

"What you said makes me feel peace. It was me who
decided to end it with Nectarios. I felt bad, so bad for
Lidia. Being in love with your Father was like a merry go
round; happy, sick, happy then sick again. When we did
not see each other for two weeks, I took my time to
think. And then, I imagined myself as Lidia - do I tell
her? No. That would ruin things for everybody. But I
could not continue, so I ended it. It was hard but I bit my
lip and closed the book. But by then I was pregnant with
this angel."

Nicola encouraged her to continue.

"In those times, having a baby without a husband was a
big *krima*, a sin. All my friends rejected me, called me a
poutana. But my sister lived in Shepparton with her

husband. I moved in with them. Alex was born in the house; she was so impatient. We survived picking fruit and doing other jobs. I worked hard for her. Your Father helped. He sent money for many years. When Alex was ready to come to Melbourne to study, we saved enough money to buy this small place. Nobody wanted to live in Northcote then. We lived through everything together, good and bad."

"Did Nectarios ever visit you after it was over?"

"Once. In Shepparton. He came two weeks before Alex was born. I did not let him come again. People in Shepparton did not judge me like in Melbourne. Your Father supported us. I could not tell Alex the truth until she was eighteen." She began crying as she reached out to her daughter.

"Mum, it's all in the past." Alex winked at Nicola as she consoled Rena.

"You were very brave Rena." said Nicola.

After dessert and coffee, Rena came to Nicola and hugged him tightly. "I hope I can make roast lamb for you again."

"I would love that Rena. Thank you for having me. It was lovely to meet you."

"And thank you for the flowers. Alex, be nice to your brother. He is the only one you have."

"Goodnight, Mum." said Alex with a kiss.

Rena shuffled off to bed.

At the sink, they cleaned up together. Alex rested an arm on Nicola's shoulder.

"Well recovered, very smooth."

"Thanks."

They drank another coffee before the conversation turned to work.

"So, they've told you to go back to boring old counselling before going back to analysing rapists and murderers?"

"Pretty much. I was forced to take leave between Dad's illness and Mum's dementia."

"Hmm. Ok."

"Hmm, what?"

"I may be able to help you. Leave it with me."

Aki looked at his email and read and re-read the offer seven times. He looked at the offer of the research and teaching position again. The room started spinning and he closed his eyes until it safe to open them again. Using low-frequency radio telescopes to look for the first stars and galaxies of the early universe less than a million years after the Big Bang. He thought of how gullible people filled their lives with religion or helping humanity beyond help, like pouring water into a cup full of holes. This was his religion, science, immutable. His impressive PhD and a strong recommendation from his supervisor landed him in the big time.

He emailed his acceptance back and waited for the read receipt. He made a checklist of things to do in the fourteen before he left for MIT, Boston.

Kondos looked at the package on his desk. Half the size of a shoebox, he gently shook it and heard something light and hard sliding in it. He opened it and stared at the single laminated card. He googled Eastern symbols and saw a match for the image on it - karma. He turned the card over and saw the words in block type capitals:

HOW MANY, PROFESSOR?

Lidia had only been back in bed ten minutes from her bathroom rendezvous when Nicola walked in. From her face, he knew she'd been on a date again. Pina confirmed with a subtle wink.

"How are you, Mum?"

"Oh caro Nicola. Molto bene."

Nicola heard angst from other residents that accompanied the dusk witching hour. He mused on the coming together of families at the end of the day in houses, replaced by illness, dependence and restriction. Here was Lidia in her pomp as she met with her man on a daily basis. She glowed where others waned until the visits of their loved ones topped up their mood. But these were mere sugar rushes that faded fast. Lidia was independent, her neural pathways bypassing decline as relived memories fooled her limbic system into thinking this was new.

"Nicola!" He chided himself for drifting away in thought.

"Sorry. What did you say?"

"Claudio, he came before."

They made small talk before Nicola tucked her in and sat
by her side for a further hour. He fell asleep. Pina woke
him at eleven p.m.

The air off Port Phillip Bay blew straight through Nicola
the next morning as he propelled his way down Beach
Road. The route was busy. The broad church of cyclists
was on show; recreational, semi-serious and pretentious
wankers took the same route to Mordialloc. The latter
presented as groups of four to six proclaiming *peloton on
your right* as they passed. Cyclists gasped for smokes or
caffeine at the bricked cafe as Nicola sat on the grass
demolishing a banana. He got up to get a short black
before heading back when he heard two sponsor heavy
riders talking.

"You're quiet, Savva. What's with you?"

"Olivia's shitty with me again. Just for a change."

Nicola's ears burned. He filtered out the peripheral noise
and kept his body from moving. Hello, Professor
Kondos.

"How's work?"

"Exam season's over. Thank Christ."

Nicola asked for a muffin from the display opposite and
asked for it to be warmed up to buy time.

Kondos leant in closer and whispered. A student got her boyfriend to call me saying I tried to grope her.

"Where do these people get off?"
 "Fucking ungrateful parasites."

Kondos shook his head. His companion suggested he had nothing to worry about and that they should push on.

Kondos was a muscular specimen with a confident gait. Nicola sized him up and was wary of getting too close. He was a little too aware of the excitement of the chase that the chance encounter provided and pulled back.

Nicola kept them in his periphery as they mounted and rode away. He soon passed them despite leaving five minutes later, overtaking them as they struggled up the rise at Ricketts Point. the mild headwind catching many. Nicola pushed on with ease to his car by the London Hotel in Port Melbourne. He arrived home to find Claudio waiting in his car out front.

"Where do you go dressed like this?"

"Riding, Zio. What does it look like?"

"You look like a condom Nicola. Anyway, I thought we should take your Mother out for a picnic. We used to go to the Botanic Gardens on weekends. It's a nice day. Hurry up. We have to have her back before four."

Lidia was in a good mood when they arrived and was anxious to know where they were going. Claudio drove while Nicola held Lidia's hand in the back seat.

Lidia stared at the lake as they sat in The Rose Pavilion. She opened the box and took out a plain roll. "Mangiate ragazzi," she said to the swans as she threw small chunks of bread against all rules like she had many times before. She enjoyed watching the pecking order as the alpha male swan filled up before allowing the others to eat. They trio shared the panini and moved onto the *torrone* and coffee from the thermos Claudio prepared.

She smiled at them both, opening her arms for a cuddle. They stayed a little longer before they returned to the car. They made no mention of Lidia's afternoon dates. They had her back and resting in bed by three-forty. Nicola swore she pretended to close her eyes like a little girl. After they left, she applied her makeup and went on another date.

On the way out, Marco introduced them to the new gerontologist. Dr Fredel had retired.

"Dr Girolamo Del Vecchio." he said in a formal tone.

Claudio and Nicola laughed as they shook hands with him. Del Vecchio was used to the joke and had long stopped taking offence. He was a tall spindly man with rolled-up sleeves and brown hair that flopped over his thick shell frames and olive face. His beard, glasses and height conferred a professorial appearance to the elderly

Italian and Greek residents. That he spoke both fluently endeared him to both groups.

"Your Mother, if I may speak from an academic perspective, is a most interesting person."

"What do you mean?" asked Nicola.

"In most cases, patients at the stage your Mother was at a month or two ago deteriorate as a faster rate. But Lidia seems to have adopted a reality that she inhabits for an hour a day. She is reliving her love affair for Nectarios; she has dates with him. I am sure she even has physical thoughts about him, physical, sexual thoughts that a young, nubile woman might have. For that half-hour, she is twenty years young again. Neither of you can stop it, nor can she. She will be suspended in this phase until either her body changes and this memory association dissolves, or something shakes her out of it. Her blood pressure is more stable than it has ever been, her cholesterol levels are lower. This reality of hers is doing her a world of good."

Nicola looked to Claudio to see if he needed any clarification.

"I understand, Nicola. The New Lidia is the Old Lidia." said Claudio.

"Y-yes." said Dr Del Vecchio, irritated by the simplicity.

27

Claudio drove the six blocks to an underground carpark. He pulled out a plastic bag from the compartment under his seat and swallowed the blue pill with water. He sat and waited in the car for fifteen minutes. He walked up the stairs and nodded to the woman behind the minimal counter. As five women came out, he began to get cold feet and got up to leave.

Then he saw her. He felt a cold sweat and had to blink to make sure he wasn't dreaming.

"Who is the last one, please."

"Laura."

Laura was petite with black hair and brown eyes. "Hi baby, come on in."

"Claudio." he said, once in the room.

Laura led him further into the room. He sat on the edge of the bed and grabbed the corners of the mattress, his veins popping out. *First-timer* thought Laura. She gauged him as sixty, maybe sixty-five. She sat next to him and rubbed his shoulders. He loosened his grip on the mattress, "Claudio. Relax. Let's shower first. Would you like that?"

He looked over her and found it difficult not to see
Morena in front of her. Her black hair, olive skin, dark
brown eyes, her proportion all matched her. She tried to
read his face and concluded he was just nervous.

He nodded and placed his hands on his knees. Mute, he
let her undress him and lead him into the double shower.
She soaped him up and rinsed him off. Claudio asked if
he could return the favour. *What a gentleman.* Of course.

From the time she put on the condom to his climax as she
rode him fifteen minutes later, her eyes never left his.
She even let him run his hands through her hair.

"Thank you." he said as he left the room.

Laura winked at him and told him to come back any
time.

Leaving the car park, his cock was hard again. He
smiled, opened the window and let the breeze blow over
him. He was hungry after his efforts. At *Ferrini*, he
ordered the fettuccine puttanesca, keeping the silly joke
to himself.

28

Four black crows flew through the open window and worked together to open Lidia's ensuite door. Lidia sat helpless in her bed calling out Nectario! Nectario! but too late as the crows lifted him limb by limb to get him off the ground and out the window. Lidia's face hardened and turned to white. Nicola ran into the room as Nectarios hovered above the bed, lunged and landed hard on his unprotected ribs against the windowsill with arms outstretched. The crows took their carrion to the sky and disappeared with their cackling laughter.

Nicola turned as he woke and was rewarded with a bolt of pain down the right side of his ribs. He turned the other way and stayed still in case he was dreaming. He tempted fate and the pain returned. He rang Alex and described the pain and the dream.

"Psychosomatic pain is pretty common Nicola. I'll pass by this afternoon. Gotta go, flat chat here."

He decided to go for a swim to see if it would pass. An hour later, the pain eased off with the gentle jets of the spa. He was still ginger and kept his movements to a minimum. He parked in front of the house and swore at the crows on his parents' windowsill. *Seriously, fuck off already.*

He shooshed the birds away and went into the garage to find Nectarios' airgun. It was pristine. He found boxes of pellets. He took two boxes into the house with the gun and stored them in the laundry cupboard for easy access. He knew this was stupid, but the pain from the dream goaded him. *Great, now I'm a sniper in wait for fucking black crows.*

He answered the phone on the second ring. Alex.

"I'm free now for a sec. How are you feeling?'

"Better, but it hurts when I turn."

"Ha! You old prick."

"You're older than me, remember?"

"Be nice to your sister."

She arrived later and they walked together to visit Nectarios, each tending a side of the grave. Nicola smiled at Alex. While he respected the unified position of Alex and Rena to never see Nectarios in the flesh, he appreciated the flipside.

"Look, I can't do anything about the past, but, I'm sorry."

"You have accepted me, well apart from that first time when you went into shock. That's enough for me. Just don't ghost me Ok? I couldn't handle that."

"I won't. Do you have a boyfriend, Alex?"

"No. Between work and Mum, there's no time."

"Are you seeing anyone?"

He thought about telling her. "Nah, long story."

She smoothed out some dirt on her side and looked at Nectarios' picture. "How are you going to tell the rest of your family about me? Or more to the point, are you?"

Nicola looked outside their new bubble and wondered how Claudio, Rita and Sia would react. He knew the first two would be problematic.

"I need time, Alex. With my Mum and everything, I need time. Nectarios' sisters are complete opposites and my uncle-"

"Are you ashamed of me, is that it?"

"Of course not. Why would you think that?"

"I wanted to hear it - that you're not ashamed."

She moved to his side and they locked arms, their shadows growing as they lingered.

Pari drove his brother to the airport. Angelo sat in the back; consoling Rita as Aki sat silent the whole way. Unaccustomed to the back seat, Angelo fidgeted to Rita's great annoyance. Aki boarded his plane on the first call, said his goodbyes and turned only once to wave, leaving Rita inconsolable. He looked forward to a role that was all consumed by looking back, before the current abomination called the human race. As the plane made its first jerking movement, he went into a cold sweat before feeling an overwhelming happiness. He was free.

Three hours in, he popped a Temazepam with some water and went for a piss. He fell asleep as the plane drifted past the international date line and over Hawaii. He dreamt of Claudia Black welcoming him to his office.

It was a cold night in second year and the house party had spilled out into the backyard after the birthday boy drunkenly blew out his candles. Anika Glasson decided to take time out and flopped out in the first bedroom she found. Nicola asked her if she was Ok and offered to sit with her. She waved him said 'shanks I'm Ok Nico-lah'. The next day, she reported being raped by the police. It had happened under their noses and the classmates closed ranks around the rapist. No one would tell Nicola and Anika was too drunk to remember. The group of friends splintered. Over the next three months, Anika sank into a dark hole of depression. Nicola persisted, but could get nothing out of her, and she eventually closed him out of her life. A week after their last conversation, she committed suicide. At the funeral, he surveyed the mourners and stopped when he saw the look on Dale Rochester's face. He noticed him earlier standing on the far right of the church and facing dead straight while everyone angled their bodies toward the coffin in respect. He didn't look once at the casket at the burial and his eyes darted when Nicola tried to make eye contact.

"Takes a lot of balls to show up to farewell a friend doesn't it?" Nicola asked Rochester as he walked to his car.

When he couldn't meet his gaze, when his other classmates looked on but didn't intervene, he knew and

drove Rochester without resistance to the nearest Police Station, where he confessed.
 The look on her face as she shut the door on him remained burned into his memory until the brain found ways to wallpaper over it. It took years for the image to leave him and now it was back; hair stuck to her face, matted with tears, her dark eyes alive but dead, distant and resigned.

Nicola looked up and saw Anika's face in negative relief against the ceiling for a further second. His eyes ached from the sudden upward movement. He looked across at the note he wrote the night before.

Call VicPol - no more.

He turned at the sound of the aark. He jumped out of bed and walked out front to be sure. *Ma vaffanculo* he said aloud to the pair of crows perched on the roof and shooed them away. He rolled up his note and threw it in the bin. He wolfed down a Nurofen with his coffee and decided to write a short note addressed to Olivia Kondos.

Fuck him, let nature take its course.

He folded the note into the square envelope and left it unsealed.

He looked up the Hawthorn East address online, saw the house's front view and left to get it over with while Kondos was at work.

He drove along Gillam St and found the neat white Edwardian weatherboard with matching picket fence. With no car in the bricked driveway, he parked three houses down. He walked to the mailbox and hooded his face from the drizzle. *Just drop it in and go.*

A curtain moved and a girl with shoulder length blonde curls clapped with excitement. "Mummy! Mail! I get it for you."

Fuck. Nicola dropped the envelope in. The front door opened when he got halfway to his car. As he looked back, a silver BMW pulled into the driveway, Kondos lowering his window and beeping his horn. Olivia rushed out to catch the girl holding the envelope to the sky, shouting 'Mailman over there Daddy' as she ran barefoot to Nicola's car. Olivia rushed to her, trainers slipping and squeaking on the wet concrete before grabbing the hand with the envelope. She read the letter, looking from it to Kondos, to Nicola standing next to his car and back to Kondos. Her body shook, eyes wide open with incredulity as she read it again. She shoved the girl, now crying, toward the house and strode back towards Kondos. She said something but Nicola couldn't make it out.

Nicola got in and pressed the accelerator hard without pulling his belt on. He missed a taxi coming the other way by less than a foot. He turned left at the T at the bottom of the hill and took the first left again before buckling in. *Harold St meets Burke Rd I'm sure.* He tried to catch the fresh green light but got caught by crossing pedestrians. His right temple throbbed, and he cursed himself for not posting the letter. *Well done, bright eyes.* Clear now and a honk from the car behind. Nicola gave it plenty and looked ahead. Car horns blared behind him, the silver of Kondos' car three maybe four cars behind, Kondos' head straining out of his window for a better view. *Find Barkers Rd* Nicola said aloud, as if navigating to a rally driver. A long line of cars queued to turn right. He changed lanes and went straight. He indicated to turn right down Mont Albert Road at the next lights. At the lights, Nicola floored it straight. Trapped five cars back, Kondos cursed as a row of cars to his left blocked the way. He spotted a gap, made the instantaneous calculation and screeched through. A parked white courier vehicle pulled out without looking. Kondos swerved to go around it. The BMW caught the wet slick of the tram lines and spun at right angles to the traffic, keeping its angle before smacking into the front of the tram hard between the driver and rear right panel, the car lifting for a moment on one side, resting inches from the pavement and a tram stop full of people. Some passengers fell after boarding but the tram held its position. The right side of Kondos' head hit his window frame hard on impact before the airbag caught him on the rebound. his skull fracturing on impact. An off-duty paramedic jumped off the tram with his son and called 000. He approached the convulsing body from the passenger side and freed the crushed right hand that tried to protect his head. His hands identified the skull fracture, bleeding well underway and kept the neck straight. The ambulance arrived five minutes later, placed Kondos in a neck brace and blared to the Epworth.

Nicola was turning down Sackville St as the collision happened.

Olivia left the girls with the next-door neighbour until her Mother could get there and drove to find Savva, the damp letter sitting text up on the passenger seat. She turned it over and gripped the wheel tight down Burke Road. The distorted BMW chassis was surrounded by policemen, paramedics and rubberneckers. She parked and ran. A policewoman stopped her.

"My husband- that's my husband's car. Where is he?!"

"Epworth. You're shaking. Let me drive you in your car, Ok?"

Nicola turned the radio on and listened to the traffic alert about the crash. A BMW sedan has hit a tram at the corner of Burke and Mont Albert Roads. He pulled over. No mention of the driver as being dead. He thought that Kondos had either given up or he had lost him. He drove back, going up Peverill St, Deepdene Rd than back down Mont Albert Rd where he parked a block away. He walked down on the opposite side of the road and bought a bottle of water from the Shell, ignoring the car and the crowd. As he walked back, he winced at the wreck and confirmed it was Kondos' car. Police were already analysing the car, their pointing and hand gestures recreating the path of the now crumpled chassis. He wondered if there was any way they would connect him to the incident. He hoped Kondos was dead. Best for all concerned.

He drove home and replayed it all in his head before getting out of the car. His pulse dipped back into double figures. He turned on the TV. The car looked worse than with his own eyes. No one could survive that. He distracted himself for the rest of the evening watching more of The Sopranos. He finished with *Whoever Did This*, rooting for Tony as he delivered Ralph Cifaretto's long overdue whacking.

31

He woke late morning to three texts from Alex.

Call me when you're free. I'm free this arvo x A

Come on sleepy head. Call me whenever.

Stop fucking around and call me.

He looked at his maze of scribbling - arrows and vectors. The diagram looked so random, yet symmetrical, each force cancelled out by another. He concluded that something would have happened in the end. Newton's third law was irrefutable. He felt for Olivia, for Petra and for any other girls whose trust and bodies Kondos had violated.

Alex let fly when she answered the phone. "What's your excuse?"

"Not now, long story. Come over at seven for dinner. I'll do a quick pasta."

He hung up before she could ask more.

Petra answered on the second try.

"I was in the shower; sorry Nicola."

"If you had plans cancel them. Be here at seven. We need to talk. It's important."

Nicola took his mind off things by preparing Lidia's pasta mista. *Penne matriciana, linguini aglio e oglio con cile* and *orecchiette alla panna*. He tried his best to keep his thoughts away from Kondos. For minutes at a time, he could as the three sauces kept his hands and brain at full capacity. He turned the sauces down for their final reduction when the doorbell rang.

He opened the door and greeted Petra. Alex was parking across the road and waved at Nicola.

"Who's she?" asked Petra with a cheeky grin.

Nicola hugged her cousin. "Definitely not what you think Petra."

Alex walked up and confusion took over. Both women looked at each other and demanded an answer from Nicola.

"Come inside. Alex. Petra. Petra. Alex."

He sat them down.

"Petra, this is Alex."

"You said that already." said Petra.

"Alex is my sister. Half-sister. Your Thio Nectario had an affair with Alex's Mother, Rena. Alex is Nectarios' daughter, my half-sister and your half cousin. Just take my word for it and for now promise me you'll keep it between us."

Petra screwed her eyes up. "When? Before you or after?"

"Before me and after they were married. Why?" replied Nicola.

"Just wondering."

They let it sink in, Alex clasping her hands together, uncertain. Petra got closer and looked into her eyes. She pulled out her phone, scrolled, and showed her a picture of a young Sia.

"You could easily be my older sister." said Petra, and hugged Alex. After some silent shock, Petra cried and then Alex, relieved and surprised at Petra's acceptance.

Alex looked at Nicola. "There's more isn't there?"

Women thought Nicola.

"Yes Nicola, we know. Spill it." said Petra.

Nicola asked Petra to recount her encounter with Kondos to Alex.

"Petra, I'm so sorry. Kondos taught me in third year. I'm a GP. I always thought he was a sleaze at Uni. He tried to ask me out once. I ignored him. One day he brushed up against me like I should be so privileged. I dug my heel into his toes and that was the end of it. I'm so sorry this happened to you. Are you Ok?"

"Better now."

They looked at Nicola, waiting for more. He was ill-equipped to explain what had happened, looking at the floor.

"Well?" said Alex, exasperated.

"Ok. I wrote a letter to drop into his mailbox this morning; Hawthorn East. When I got there, his daughter, a five, six-year-old girl spotted me from the window and got excited thinking I was the mailman. I dropped the letter in the mailbox and walked to my car as quick as I could, but then Kondos turns up in his car. I thought he'd be at work. His wife comes, reads the letter. Then I drove off and Kondos and I had a car chase. We got to Burke Rd, and I thought I'd lost him, but he was a few cars behind me. Turns out he crashed into a tram on the corner of Mont Albert Rd. The car's a complete write-off."

"A car chase?" asked Petra, mouth open.

"A silver BMW?" asked Alex. Nicola nodded. "It was on the news last night. No way he survived that."
"That's what I'm thinking. And hoping." said Nicola.

"Can we find out if he's dead?" asked Petra. Her mouth curled up and made Nicola feel uncomfortable.
 "Why would you drop the letter off in person?" asked Alex.

"Don't know - and yes it was a bad idea."

"When exactly did you realise it was a bad idea?"

"Well clearly somewhere between the appearance of the BMW and now. Pretty much that whole stretch of time, OK?"

Nicola heaved and resumed.

"Point is, I don't know if anyone witnessed the chase or my car, me or my number plate. I was well clear at the time of the collision. I didn't know about it until the radio traffic alert came on. I went back the long way to confirm it for myself- "

"Wait. You went back?" asked Alex.

"Did you want to be caught?" chimed in Petra.

"Well if you were in my shoes would you not have gone back to make sure it was him?"

"I wouldn't have been at his house in the first place."
said Alex.

"I had planned to call the police, but I had a dream. Anyway, I changed my mind."

"A dream."

"Yes, a dream - a friend from Uni was raped and committed suicide three months later. I dreamt of her face and I wanted Kondos to lose everything."

Alex grabbed Nicola hard by the shoulder. "I'm only pissed off with you because you got involved in the drama of the scenario instead of sending the letter. That would have been enough. Once proven, she would have left him with nothing, and he would be in jail. Now it's rather more complicated."

"Assuming she gave him up when she read the letter." said Nicola.

Petra looked at them both. "This has to stay with the three of us."

Alex and Nicola nodded.

The pasta needed a quick reheat and the three sat, the food lifting their mood.

"To new family." toasted Petra.

They clinked before Alex turned to Nicola. "What was in the letter? You left that bit out."

Nicola squirmed, before sipping some water and reciting it almost as an apology.

Dear Olivia,
Your husband rapes female students in return for pass grades.
Apologies,
Concerned Citizen.

"Nice touch." said Alex. "So, she would attack him with the scenario the letter describes and draw it out of him. You are quite the psychologist. Well played. And a good cook too. I must find you a wife to keep you out of trouble." She planted a kiss on Nicola's cheek, leaving a juicy pasta stain behind.

"Yep, always wanted a sister." said Nicola, half crying, half laughing.

"Me too!" said Petra.

After midnight, Nicola's thoughts wandered again to Kondos. He had no sympathy for him, but a default level of guilt. He wondered what it must have been like in those milliseconds when Kondos thought his life was over, and how lucky it was that no one else was injured or killed. Far better to have his conduct and character given due scrutiny in a court of law and receive the appropriate punishment. *Far harder to prove it* said the countering voice in his head. Judges were soft, and he had seen justice cave into lawyers wrangling. This one was outside anyone's control and that thought bothered him.

32

Petra thought about Kondos and wondered which hospital he was in so she could laugh at his disfigured face. She thought it would be fun to examine his MRIs and CAT scans to map the distortions his brain had experienced from the impact. *I hope you die* she said aloud as she turned the last corner before home.

Alex was angry with Nicola for being so careless. She reflected whether Nectarios was as careless. Her mind wandered to whether her existence was down to Nectarios' carelessness. Whenever she pondered her existence, how she got here, she held onto the same thought, an affirmation she returned to from time to time.

No self-pity, Alex. You're here because you're here.

33

Olivia's athletic form left an imprint on the waiting room couch as she waited for what seemed forever. She flicked through the various fashion magazines. When she had exhausted them, she drew the note from her pocket. She read it again three times before putting it away. She wanted her husband to come through just so she could show it to him and see the face she got back. She would know in an instant. Her fists clenched hard and then her heart quickened. She touched her fingertips and practised breathing: in for four and out for eight. Her pulse dropped again.

A doctor shuffled over after three and a half hours and introduced himself as Naresh. As they moved to a quiet corner of the waiting area, Olivia wondered if this was how they announced the dead, like in the movies.

"Olivia, we have stopped the bleeding. He had significant skull fractures from the impact. The pressure in his brain was very high but we think we have got it down as low as we can for now. He's breathing with assistance."

"Is he awake?"

"No, and he won't be for quite a few hours. I don't know what state he'll be in when he wakes. We'll scan him and see."

Olivia chewed on those words and became detached from the conversation.

"Olivia, are you OK?"

"Yes, sorry Doctor. I'm a bit tired, as you must be. Thank you."

Olivia pressed the doctor's forearm a little harder than she meant to. She turned and ran to her car. She let her tears go then, let them sting warm as thoughts ran through her head. Thoughts that sounded like other peoples' voices.

Stand by him.
You can work through this.
Why did he go after him as a man possessed?
Because he's a rapist.

Now she had to go home to answer questions and pretend she cared. From her daughters, from her Mother, her friends, his parents, his colleagues, police, neighbours.

So, this is hell.

Olivia's Mother emerged as she opened the gate. Maya, eight and Grace, five stood behind in their pyjamas and robes. "We're all OK," she told them both and drew a large lung full of air before she tucked her girls into bed. She told them that Daddy had gone away for a while, but he would be back when he was better. It was the best she could come up with.

The tube in Kondos' skull monitored intracranial pressure.

If he were here with a group of students, he would explain with clear precision the anatomical features at play. He would link the functional defects to the structural damage. He would explain with great authority that the brain has the consistency of soft butter, bathed by fluid and encased in a skull with smooth and sharp contours defining its interior topography. He would observe the students' faces. He read faces well. But here, he was the subject. Besides the tube in his skull, he had a trach to breathe with and a feeding tube to eat with. Nurses came and went, took blood, measured and recorded.

Olivia sat across from two people in a boardroom. A tall gangly, goateed man who appeared uncomfortable in a tie greeted her. A short woman with glasses, corseted in a navy suit sat next to him.

"Mrs Kondos,-" the man began.

"Please, Olivia."

"Olivia I'm Rufus Stagan and this is Erica Niles. The Faculty of Medicine has asked us to handle the transition of the Anatomy Department after your husband's unfortunate accident. We are sorry to hear of his injuries. Your husband will not be in a position to continue his role in the near future. We will be replacing him as a temporary measure until we know more. His entitlements-"

"Near future? Let's face facts. He won't be back to teach anatomy. When can I clear his office?"

The man and woman looked at each other and nodded in agreement. This was unexpected.

"We can take you-" began Rufus Stagan. Erica put her hand up and smiled.

"I'll take you, Olivia. We can go over your husband's entitlements in the circumstances of his injury. Then I'll take you to collect his items. Is that Ok? As you are his financial and medical power of attorney that should not pose any issues."

Olivia nodded. Erica Niles looked at Rufus Stagan who excused himself. "I wish your husband a strong recovery Olivia."

Alone, the women went over the financial details and cover arising from the accident. He had leave entitlements, insurance and was entitled to have his annual leave and pro-rata redundancy paid out in full. They made short work of the official paperwork and walked to Kondos' office. Outside the door, they stopped. She handed Olivia her number.

"In normal circumstances, I'm supposed to supervise anybody clearing an office, but I'm only a few doors down so I'll leave you to it. I'll have some boxes brought in. Call me when you're ready."

"Thanks."

Olivia surveyed the office, an L-shaped desk with many drawers, and a wide, tall bookcase loomed behind it. Leather armchairs sat near a large window looking over Grattan St. She counted well over twenty framed certificates, awards and fellowships on the walls and realised the enormity of the job. She decided to start on the drawers, opening them with Kondos' keys and emptying the contents into the provided document boxes. Exam papers, papers to be peer-reviewed and pad after pad of scribbled notes filled the draws. At the bottom of the last drawer she lifted four folders out. She tried to lift the last one when the metal corner snagged on whatever was below it. The folder finally gave way before Olivia noticed a metal sheet clipped into grooves on the sides of the drawer caused the snag. She tapped the metallic surface with her nail and heard a hollow echo. She found a ruler and tried to jam open the sheet. She went through a ruler and two pens before she found a metal letter opener engraveded with SK. She stabbed the edges down on one side to break the clasps from their grooves. She then removed the sheet from the other side, taking care not to cut herself. She looked at the contents and remembered a conversation from a few months ago. Olivia wanting to back up all their photos onto USBs, Kondos scoffing.

"Why bother storing info on USB sticks? They're too easy to lose. The cloud's the best way to go."

Olivia's mind went to the worst as she looked at them. She gathered up the sticks strewn along the base, all black, all 64GB and lay them on the desk. Booting up her laptop, she placed one in and clicked on the single file named Cheree Rivers dating back fifteen months. The video was out of focus before clearing after a few seconds. Kondos spoke to a blonde woman, the back of his head facing the camera. She scrubbed the video forward, and she could only watch ten seconds of Kondos fucking her from behind. Despite the grainy footage, the panic was clear on the girl's face, her eyes wide with fright as her husband held her hands tight in one of his large hands, the other holding her shoulder blade down. Olivia shut the laptop, making a clanging noise, and knocked over a pair of books onto the floor. As Erica Niles' hurried footsteps echoed down the corridor, the audio still came through the laptop and Olivia forgot where the volume control was. She yanked the USB out from and shoved it and the other USBs into her bag.

"What was that noise?" asked Erica. "Is everything Ok?"

"Yes, thanks Erica. I dropped one of his books on the floor. I had forgotten how heavy these anatomy texts were."

"Ok then." Erica walked back to her office.

Olivia breathed in deeply and thought. How did he record these?

Textbooks said Olivia to herself as she looked behind her. Lots of textbooks.

She moved onto the bookcases, almost slipping off the tall library ladder before reaching the third row. She narrowed her eyes and saw the brief reflection. A-ha. A tattered hard copy of *Moore and Dalley's Essential Clinical Anatomy* sat with a small lens poking about a third of the way down the spine. Olivia descended and sat where Cheree had sat and confirmed for herself that the lens could not have been seen. She climbed the ladder again and looked back down. The angle was perfect for its intended, perverted purpose. She pulled the book towards her, descended the ladder and opened it up. The book was hollowed out. A small video camera had been inserted inside the thick cardboard casing; its pages neatly excised.

Fucking prick never took video of his daughters.

Olivia sat in one of the leather armchairs and looked out over the groups of students, like bees on the street below. She looked further and saw the tall CBD buildings and made a decision. She finished in one last burst of energy, called out for Erica and asked for a trolley to move the boxes to the car that were personal and left the rest behind. A tall man in blue overalls helped her fill the boot of her car.

After putting the girls to bed, she steeled herself to look at the contents of the remaining UBSs. She wanted to be in no doubt. The pattern was the same; a distressed female student asking for more time or special consideration followed by Kondos suggesting they help each other or risk repeating a year of study. Kondos drawing out the students' stress to make his perverted outcome the only choice left. The last USB was titled Petra. Olivia gasped as the student sprang to life, surprising Kondos with a kick to the groin, sending him to the floor clutching them before running out of view.

Olivia counted seventeen USBs, seventeen girls in all. She copied the contents onto a larger single USB stick she had cleared, double bagged and hid them in her separate parts of her secret wardrobe compartment. She thought over all her options again and decided all were ugly, but some were less so.

She stripped and remade her bed, then gathered all the pictures in the bedroom and shredded those with his face. After stuffing the sheets and photos in the bin, she knocked on her Mother's door. She looked up from her bed, put down her book and made room for her daughter.

"What happened, Bella?"

"Mum, Savva had an affair. That man was leaving me a note to tell me."

"What do you want to do? I'm behind you whatever you decide to do."

"I'm divorcing him."

"With him in hospital like this?"

"Mum, I know you won't say it, but you were right. He was and is a bad person."

"I didn't like him when you brought him home. Lucky your Father isn't here - he would have taken him apart, joint by joint. Just remember one thing - it's not your fault, Olivia. Don't blame yourself."

"I'm selling the house and we're moving back to Sydney."

Her Mother stifled a smile. "Are you sure?"

"You know I am. I resisted moving because of, I can't even bring myself to say his name, his career. Can you stay with us a little longer until we move?"

"Of course, darling, as long as you need. I have no one to go back to. Stay with me until you find your own place."

"We'll start fresh up there. The girls are still young, and they will make new friends."

Olivia hugged her Mother. She decided to take the girls to visit their Father.

36

On his third visit, Claudio asked if Laura was her real name.

"I can't tell you my real name, Claudio."

"You know mine."

She became irritated. "And I believe you. But I can't tell you mine. Shall we?"

Claudio closed his eyes and whispered *Morena mia* as she rode him. He showered. As he dressed, she asked him who Morena was.

"My wife. She passed away a long time ago." said Claudio as he walked towards the door.

"Do I look like her?"

He stopped and their eyes met. Claudio hesitated before replying. "A little bit, same colour hair." he said and trudged his way out.

The painting of Morena Claudio had done for her off a black and white photo used to take up space in a spare bedroom. She refused to pose for it and demanded it be out of the way. The day after her funeral, he mounted it above his bed, its ornate metal square frame almost half the bed's width. The artist had used varying shades of reds in the background that reflected onto her olive skin as she faced left, her look pensive yet happy. Her natural, plump lips pouted without her even trying, the shadowing on the right side of her nose showing her reflective nature, her hair parted off centre because she liked it that way, her black curls collecting under her perfect chin and over her favourite crimson dressing gown.

Claudio stood at the end of the bed and apologised to her. He strained to see her lips move the way they did when she expressed an opinion, but nothing moved. He watched the reflection in the mirror opposite as he lay down, transfixed until he fell asleep, his bedside lamp still on.

37

Lidia got up for her regular triste. Since she had moved rooms, her visitor had arrived a little late. Today though he arrived on time and held out flowers for her. His hair was ruffled from the rush.

"Ma come sei bella oggi Lidia." How beautiful you are today Lidia. His strong arms caressed her. The warmth ignited her body, warmer than that prison of a bed. He smelled her hair and cooed into her hair.

A loud knock on the door interrupted them. She ignored it and returned to the man's tender nibbles at her ear.

Another knock. Louder.

"Lidia, time for your medication." An unfamiliar voice, flat and low. Now the knocks came in pairs.

Pina knew to wait until she returned to bed before coming with her medications. The nurse she had changed shifts with didn't bother reading the handover notes. Her man disappeared like a vapour. Lidia was used to a gradual goodbye and her face contorted. She turned away from the fury in the mirror and yelled in a guttural voice she didn't recognise.

"Ma che cazzo vuoi troia ritardata? Non ti capita che mi sono occupata ?!"

What the fuck do you want, you retard? Can't you tell
I'm busy?!

"Come on, Lidia."

Lidia stormed through the door with hands outstretched.
Her hands grabbed the nurse's throat, the blue veins
around her knuckles dilated. Though a large woman, the
nurse was no match for Lidia in this frenzied state. She
tried to press the buzzer on her belt clip but failed and
yelled until help came, her breathing becoming
shallower. Marco separated them as an orderly held her,
another nurse injecting the sedative to Lidia's arm.

She resisted but was eventually restrained on her bed
until she went limp. The nurse shook off all help and
stormed outside to regroup. Marco would rip through her
when the dust settled. Dr Del Vecchio looked on.

The next day, Lidia sat up in bed facing the bathroom
door, but didn't make her habitual visit. On the third
morning, the cleaning staff discovered food in the
strangest of places. The nurses checked her weight. She
had dropped four kilos in less than a fortnight. Dr Del
Vecchio ordered full bloods and an MRI. Marco looked
for Nicola's number before Del Vecchio persuaded him
to wait until they had all the information to make a
diagnosis. Informing loved ones too early often did more
harm and anxiety than good.

Pina chatted with Lidia until the orderlies from the
hospital next door arrived. She smiled as they made

small talk. Pina found her conversation more disjointed than usual. She had stopped talking about Nicola or Claudio.

With easy access to the adjoining hospital's imaging, Marco organised for Lidia to be wheeled in her bed. She asked Pina to hold her hand and smiled as the lights passed over her face. Bloods taken, Lidia received her Propofol.

She passed through the huge metal tube. After a short while, Pina was accompanied her back to her room. She woke up as they entered her room. Sitting bolt upright, she shivered.

"I'm cold, open the curtain so the sun can come in please, Pina."

"Of course, Lidia."

As the sun hit her body, she fell asleep again and curled up into a semi-foetal position facing the sun. Lidia's body jerked a few times before she settled. Pina placed the blanket over her, moving her fringe away so the sun could still hit her face and shoulders.

Lidia at the beach with Nectarios. They preferred Beaumaris where the trees gave some shade. Lidia with her towel facing the sun while Nectarios mouthed *ti voglio bene* opposite her. I love you.

Lidia half opened her eyes. Nectarios' face hovered in front of her. *Non come ti voglio io,* she responded with a whisper. Not as much as I love you.

38

Dr Ian Franz reviewed Lidia's MRI. The left frontal lobe showed a white mass of an oval shape about 3cm x 1cm x 2cm. He played the mouse around it and saw it was fairly well defined. Franz called Del Vecchio to confer and asked him to email the symptoms he had noticed in Lidia. He sent the list across for Franz to tick off. Colleagues found the cross-referencing method he used unusual, but it complemented the amazing imaging technology at his disposal. He believed strongly in the central tenet of matching anatomy with function. The symptoms matched the frontal lobe lesion: irregular behaviour, delusions, aggression, variable appetite, recent weight loss.

He read through the blood profile an hour later. He underlined GFAP 0.16g/L (normal <0.05g/L) and rang Del Vecchio.

"We have a progressive frontal lobe glioma."

Del Vecchio winced at the difficulties of the situation.

"Chemo's not an option I presume."

"Only if the family wants to end her in instalments. The only option is to go in and get out as much as we can. Chemo can cause short term cognitive damage but how much is dementia and how much is this growth? There isn't a lot of data on chemo on pre-existing dementia patients."

"It wasn't there in her MRI a year ago."

"So we know it's aggressive. When can we meet the family?"

"They don't know we've done all these investigations."

Irritated, Franz grunted. "We need to move. Bring them up to speed and we'll meet tomorrow."

39

It took Laura two days to decide whether to accept
Claudio's invitation to dinner, longer again for Claudio
to get the courage to ask. The thought of him at sixty-six
asking a thirty-year-old woman out to dinner seemed
ludicrous. He expected her to refuse and not let him see
her again. Now, as he sat in a restaurant with her, he tried
his best to keep his composure, forget the age difference
and enjoy himself.

"Are you Ok, Claudio?"

"It has been years since I've been out for dinner with a
woman. I know, I know, it's only dinner but you
understand. People are looking at me."

"We could be Father and daughter for all they know.
What do you care?"

"Is that supposed to make me feel better?"

"Look, it's nice to be out with someone for a casual
dinner. Now before we order, I'm paying my share." said
Laura

"No, please. I insist, I invited you. It's only dinner; a way
for me to say thank you."

"For what?"

"What we do makes me feel better." he said in a quieter voice, pointing to his head.

"I'm happy for you."

"I do not expect anything in return. You probably have a boyfriend already, yes?"

"Not that it matters, but I do - because this is only dinner, correct?"

"Yes."

Laura sipped her wine and smiled. "So, tell me about Morena. I'm curious. Do you have a picture?"

"I used to, then it became too painful. Her face is here, always." he said, pointing to his head again.

"I can imagine. Tell me about her."

"We saved enough money for a holiday. One minute we were packed for Italy, the next she had breast cancer. Three months from the day we were supposed to fly, she died. The chemotherapy made her last month a nightmare. She suffered more pain than any person should have to bear. We could not have children and we accepted this, but we chose a selfish, happy life together. God had other ideas."

Dinner came and broke the conversation. Claudio became uncomfortable about sharing too much about Morena and found it hard to talk about Laura's work.

"Do you have family nearby?"

"We don't talk." said Laura, her hands crossed in front of her.

Claudio moved to more comfortable small talk. They left without dessert after overindulging on pasta. She kissed him on the cheek and thanked him for a lovely night, before whispering into his ear.

"By the way, my real name is Gabriella. Keep it to yourself and don't use it at my work, Ok?"

"Sure, Laura."

She made a shh sign over her lips and smiled.

He offered to walk her to her car, but she pointed to her car just four spots away. He walked to his and hummed 'Buona sera, signorina, buona sera, it is time to say goodnight to Napoli.'

Across the road, Ivan Constantin seethed in the dark of his car. He started the ignition as Claudio got into his car. As he edged out, an SUV appeared to his right to reverse into the space behind. Ivan got out and smacked his large meaty hand onto the car's bonnet. The driver of the SUV took one look at Ivan's face and drove away.

Nicola waited for Claudio in the car park. He rang the Epworth as he presumed it to be the nearest hospital to the accident. Posing as a police officer from the accident scene, he spoke to a doctor who detailed the extent of his injuries. He would recover and suffered no significant brain injury. He again thought that his death would have been the best for everyone, not least his young daughters.

He ambushed Claudio as he arrived.

"Where have you been? I rang and rang last night."

"I wasn't feeling well and went to bed early."

"Since when?"

"Anyway, what is wrong?"

Nicola scanned his face for a further second and let it go.

Claudio's face screwed up. "What?"

"I don't know. Let's go."

Marco ushered them into Dr Del Vecchio's office and introduced them to Dr Franz, not as an oncologist but as a physician. Marco recounted the confrontation with the nurse.

"Lidia lost six kilos last month. Pina found her hiding food in strange places, nothing eaten. We did some tests," said Marco.

"We did full blood tests," said Dr Del Vecchio, "and I asked Dr Franz from next door to do an MRI."

Dr Franz took over. "I'm sorry but Lidia has cancer."

Claudio gripped Nicola's leg. Nicola fixated on one of Dr Del Vecchio's medical posters on the wall opposite: The Anatomy of the Brain and Skull. The sides bulged out like a pin cushion. Once it stopped, he turned to the three men.

"Frontal lobe glioma?"

"Yes. How-"

"Don't worry. Go on, please." Nicola pressed.

"It is three centimetres long and from the blood tests, it is likely to grow and could spread elsewhere in the brain. Our best option is to operate and remove as much as we can as it is surgically accessible. Chemotherapy will worsen Lidia's mental state if it doesn't kill her. Studies aren't conclusive on chemotherapy in patients with dementia, but I am certain she will deteriorate."

"Would you be doing the operation?"

"The neurosurgeon I work with will operate but I'll be assisting, yes. Should we get things going?"

"I need five minutes with Mum please." said Nicola as turned towards Claudio.

They walked along the corridor. Before Lidia's room, Claudio sat on the couch and took deep breaths. "You go first."

Nicola's mind filled with crows, the image of a ravaged Nectarios. He looked at the ordinary walls, the ordinary floor, dull spaces where we were forced to make extraordinary decisions. He sucked in a deep breath and walked in. Lidia was asleep again, facing the window. Pina walked over.

"She's sleeping a lot lately. Ever since her lover went away." Pina explained the break in routine and the attack on the nurse and apologised.

"No apology necessary, Pina. She has cancer in her frontal lobe."

Pina came from the classical, efficient mould of nurses, but here she found it hard not to cry. She patted Nicola on the back. Nicola cried it out, and Pina ushered him outside her room.

"Let it out. There's no award for being stoic."

As Nicola left the room, Lidia stirred, shielded her eyes from the sun and turned the other way.

"Non piangere, piccolino, ti carezza mamma tua," she whispered as she lifted the blanket over her cold shoulder. Don't cry, little one, mummy's here to hold you.

Nicola saw Claudio sitting on the oak tree bench through the window and let him be. He walked back to Marco's office.

"Ready when you are, Dr Franz."

Claudio put his arm around his nephew as he joined him on the bench. Where he couldn't face his sister, Nicola showed the maturity and strength Claudio wished he had. As a child, Nicola had always gravitated to Claudio and Morena and felt closest to them. Rita was especially put out by their mutual affection while blind to Angelo's old school ways. It didn't exactly make him a model uncle. Sia's late husband, Achilles, fell somewhere in between but had died too soon.

"You are braver than I have ever been, Nicola."

Nicola felt as buoyed as he could be at the moment by his uncle's approval. But in spite of that welled up and put out his hands like scales weighing up surgery against leaving it be.

"If we leave her as she is, she dies slowly. Three, six months? If we operate, she lives longer, and we risk not knowing her again."

"Or she may spend more time with us. We take what we can."

"Or she could die in surgery."

"And one of us could get hit by a tram crossing the road tomorrow. There is no easy decision Nicola."

"Why are you Mr Positivo all of a sudden? Your voice sounded different this morning. What's going on with you?"

Claudio looked him in the eye. "I am taking Lexapro."

For years Nicola had urged him to see his doctor about his depression. Only Claudio denied it.

"Bravo. I'm proud of you."

"And why are you so *moosh* these days?"

The dialect expression came from Claudio's region, meaning sour mouth. Nicola hadn't heard it in years and in spite of himself cracked a smile.

"I don't know how to describe it."

"You ask me, you have too much time to think. Troppo analitica."

Nicola nodded.

"You need to work again. I know you don't need the money, but a routine is good. Life burns, Nicola. Your skin, it grows back. Hiding from routine only makes you sick."

Nicola's pulse quickened. He breathed in for four and out for eight and repeated. He couldn't disagree but having a routine with his Mother this way didn't sit right with him.

"Do you think Lidia would like you stewing like sugo until she dies?"

Claudio was right, thought Nicola. Waiting for the next morbid event to happen so he could react to it veered on unhealthy. He needed some routine for his own mental health.

Claudio reflected that the time with Laura/Gabriella was good for him. It stopped him thinking about morbid things himself and made him feel vital. He began to think clearly for the first time in years.

Fatigue caught up with Nicola and he went to bed early. He cursed himself when he woke at 4:15 the next morning, unable to fall back to sleep.

41

Petra walked into the Epworth Hospital posing as a family member of Kondos. Visitors were now permitted, despite Kondos not being able to talk for more than a minute. He used a whiteboard and a couple of markers to communicate when he got tired. Olivia brought in Grace and Maya and Grace the one time. The five minutes passed too fast. He met Olivia's eyes twice and twice she looked away. Her kiss on the cheek felt cold and hesitant, a token gesture for the benefit of the girls. His brother Gerry came in three times, each visit half as long as the one before. They were hardly close, and the accident did little to rekindle any brotherly love. His Mother came every day for the first five days before even she tired and came every other day. His Father passed five years ago. The few other relatives came out of the silent obligation that came with being Greek, usually once and at the worst possible time.

Petra found the room, saw Kondos sleeping and heard the sound of the oxygen machine humming its low rhythm. She passed the sink and read his chart. His next medications were due at 4pm. The monitor read 3:41 pm. She approached the bed and whispered. *Savva, Savva...*

He stirred and motioned for the bed to go up at his end, mistaking Petra for a nurse.

Sure. She adjusted the bed in two short sharp jolts that made him grimace as he sat up, the blood rushing to his head. She pushed the corded remote control out of reach. The tramadol played havoc with his vision and he strained to focus on her.

When she came closer, he knew her and froze. She pulled up a chair with a view of the door in case anyone came in.

"Professor Kondos, good afternoon. I passed without your 'help', thanks very much. Those questions on renal structure and Willis' circle? Nailed them both. But I'm curious. How many others were there?"

Kondos tried to sit up straighter but struggled.

"Chop, chop then, just a rough figure. Use your hands if you can't talk. Will you ever be able to talk again Savva? Will you ever be able to pray on anxiety in that decorated office of yours?"

Kondos stared past her. Petra steered him back with a kick of the bed. "Look at me, you sick fuck."

She lowered her tone. "Don't be so modest now, Professor. It's not because of your unfortunate accident, I'm sure, but because there were so many. Have Olivia and the girls been in yet? Do they know Daddy dearest is a rapist?"

Kondos' eyes widened, and his breathing quickened. She dismissed his shock with a wave of her hand.

"Don't worry, it was easy to find out. Maybe if I could see your scans, I could read out the damaged parts of your brain, the cracked aspects of your skull. Then, I could relate them to your functional defects, like a Golden Book for Arseholes." She walked around and looked at the bandage on the right side of his skull.

"How lucky for you that the temporal bone took the impact. Just four, five millimetres further anteriorly, on the sphenoid bone, and you'd be worm food by now. How's it healing?"

She tapped the area hard with the end of her index finger and pain cannoned through his head and down the back. He closed his eyes, willing it to stop. His breathing struggled and he went into arrhythmia. He let his head rest back to slow his breathing and get his heart back into sinus rhythm as he tried to ride out the pain. Petra read BP 145/100 and pulse of 110 on his monitor. She looked him in the eye one more time, said *time to pay*, speared him with her smile, then walked out. Ten seconds later, the tone sounded for the nurse as his pulse passed 160 bpm.

42

Alex arrived a couple of minutes late for the weekly practice meeting. Dr Hercules Orestiadis, or H to his staff, liked his meetings. He bribed his staff with coffee and pastries, his short, rotund form a testament to the frequency of them. All six doctors, two nurses and seven admin staff waited. H scratched his bald spot and adjusted his round glasses, before clearing his throat with all the love of the dramatic.

"Last week, I bought the house next door."

Mouths dropped and only the clink of a spoon on a coffee mug on the table broke the silence. He rode the wave of surprise and continued.

"There will be more room and we'll be incorporating a multidisciplinary clinic with us. Dentist, Physio, Pathology, Psychology and an Endocrinologist for our diabetic cohort. Cramped is not the word to describe our current situation I can tell you, myself included. I will make provisions for a back office and a larger staff room, too. We move in four weeks. Any questions?"

The prospect of larger office space elicited profound relief from the staff. They had said it as a joke when the FOR-SALE sign went up that they should buy it. H acted before any parasite developers put up a ghastly Lego block of flats. After the meeting, Alex pulled him aside.

"You sprung that on us, didn't you?"

"Happy with the news then, Alex?"

"Yes, yes, overjoyed. Would you like a psychologist fluent in Greek and Italian and great with older people?"

"Don't tease me, Alex."

"Would I do that to you, H?"

"Oh Alex, is there anything you can't do?"

43

Nicola came up on Alex's phone as she picked it up to dial him.

"I was about to call you."

"I saved you the trouble. What were you going to ring me about?"

"My clinic is moving into the house next door to make room for some allied health people. We need a psych and I want you with us.

"Me?"

"What are you doing with your days anyway? I'm sure you're not hard up but some routine would do you good."

That word again. Routine.

"You wanted bread and butter counselling. I offer you bread and butter counselling."

"Ok then."

"Don't be too effusive in your appreciation."

"No, look, I'm sorry Alex. I am grateful."

"But you won't come?"

"I didn't say that."

"Did you enjoy it, the police work?"

"Enjoy isn't the right word, intellectually engaged is probably more accurate. I assessed criminals and prepared behavioural evaluations. I also helped examine crime scenes from a psychological perspective."

"Sounds light and airy. Why do you want to be back in that environment?"

"It's more frustrating being outside and seeing it happen than being part of it."

"Do you feel you have to prove yourself or something?"

"My mind is best occupied I suppose. Pitch it to me, what's your demographic?"

"Garden variety immigrants, their damaged kids, hipsters, corporate types, some students. Plenty of fertile material for you to work with. You won't be twiddling your thumbs and you'd be taking a huge load off our GPs."

"Gee don't make it sound too enticing."

"As an added bonus we'd be working together."

"In that case, I'm in. When can we start?"

"Brilliant. We don't move for two or three weeks but next week we can walk through. I'll make sure you get the best room."

44

Kondos still relied on the ventilator but could sit up at forty-five degrees. His brain hurt when he tried to read, and his vision went double if he read for too long. He began eating solid food again without the feeding tube. His sense of taste was returning. He was practising looking from the hands on his watch to the building opposite his room when the girls raced into his room.

Grace bumped into the bed announcing her win. She hugged her Father and Maya piled on top. Olivia trailed behind and pulled a chair a metre away from the bed. She acknowledged him by raising her eyebrows and pursing her lips as she sat.

The girls took in the view across the Yarra before Olivia told them to tell Dad about their new teachers and classmates. Leaving the -dy off Daddy made it sound foreign, like a distant relative to be tolerated. He searched her eyes for something and registered only contempt. The blue-green of her iris was now mixed with a tinge of brown and she couldn't look at him for more than a second or two. After a few minutes, Kondos's head began to throb and he tried his best to be patient. Maya rolled her eyes as Grace took her time telling her story. Olivia asked them to go to the toilet before they left. Olivia got up and bent close to Kondos' left ear.

"Listen carefully. You will not see me nor the girls again. After searching for reasons why you should, I can't find any. We are no more. My lawyer will send you divorce papers and papers for agreed custody of the girls to me. The house is up for sale. I will give you ten percent of the house and your entitlements. I'm not a total bitch, but I need the money to raise the girls without you. This is your doing. Try and butt heads with me and you will regret it." She waved a USB as proof. "I have all seventeen from that secret compartment of yours, the hidden camera too." she whispered. "Are we clear?"

He went white and his bedside equipment beeped an urgent tone as his pulse raced.

"Do you understand?" she repeated, louder this time.

He finally met her eyes, pursed his lips and nodded in agreement.

She turned on her heels and changed back to loving Mummy, asking the girls to wave bye-bye.

Kondos looked out the window again and thought it was just as well he couldn't walk yet. He would have given anything at that moment to be able to jump out the window onto Bridge Road below and end it all.

45

Nicola lay in his bed, his head swirling with Lidia, Kondos, work. He decided to meditate and expunge his worries, if only for a short while. Meditation's bullshit he once said when one of Nectarios' nurses suggested it to him. He popped on Brian Eno's 'Neroli' and began. As his mind relaxed, his Father's last conversation with him cut in and drowned out the ambient tones. Clearing space in his head only allowed past conversations and other thoughts to enter, like bouncers letting people into a nightclub when others left.

"Nicola, I haven't got much time left."

"How do you know?"

When Nectarios spoke in scientific terms he reverted to English. He liked graphs.

"If you graph me, the y-axis is me, my strength. The x-axis is time. OK? Every month since I have cancer, I drop by half, so if you imagine each month...one hundred percent, fifty, twenty-five etc. This is me."

"But Dad that formula means you never reach zero."

Nectarios winked and clicked his tongue as he did whenever he had a moment of inspiration.

"This formula never reaches zero, but God realises I cannot tolerate or survive past five, four percent. He then gives me peace. This upsets you I know, but I am OK knowing this."

"Please, Dad. Don't."

"Nicola, I have made a life where others chose to stay. I met the most beautiful woman on earth. We made you. We have never lived in poverty. We have enjoyed life and been fortunate. I don't know what is coming when I am taken away. Where do I go? I don't pretend to know. All the religion in the world cannot answer that question."

"And Mum?"

Nectarios' eyes narrowed even further, and his pale face turned an angry red. Tears came and ran over his sunken cheekbones, sinking into the wrinkles of his dry skin, coursing like tidal water through furrows in the sand.

"I have been robbed of my time with her. Not time even to go through this together. If there is a God, I will complain about this," his last words.

As he tried to wipe the tears away for his Father, imminent death showed in every small patch of pale skin and prominent veins. He held his hand with light pressure in case he caused him pain.

The music over, Nicola held his head in his hands. He sat
up and looked around to make sure he wasn't at his
Father's bedside and lay down again. *Well, that went
well.* he said aloud.

Alex introduced Nicola to H.

"Hercules Orestiadis, but H is fine for future." the bow a little over the top, especially for a man so spherical in stature.

They walked through the house where H gave Nicola the choice of three rooms. The first one faced a garden where some imposing bird of paradise dominated the view. Lidia loved her bird of paradise and though modest in size, the room felt comfortable.

"This will be fine, H."

"But there are two more. You have first choice."

"No need, this is perfect."

Claudio sat with head and clasped hands pointing at the carpet. The hexagonal pattern of the weave entranced him as he tried to shut out the conversation going on around him.

Dr Priya Somasundaram, a well-credentialed neurosurgeon who specialised in brain cancers, sat undeterred by the expectations and anxieties of the families she consulted before every surgery. She learned early in her career the art of detaching herself from the emotions at play and staying with the facts. Despite her high peer regard, jealous colleagues ridiculed her throughout her training. Some gave her the nickname of The Ice Pick. Claudio whispered to Nicola as she looked through Lidia's notes and scans.

"È piccola, no?"

"Shh." Nicola also thought she looked like a girl starting high school, but trusted Dr Franz's recommendation.

Del Vecchio and Franz joined them to discuss pre-op and post-op care and expectations. The list of possible adverse complications made Nicola's head hurt. Stroke, epilepsy, seizures, thrombosis, heart failure. Nicola asked how many cases like his Mother's she had done.

"Many, but they're all different, which makes for interesting work. I have Lidia booked in first thing tomorrow, seven a.m."

"And her state of mind?"

"This type of surgery in patients with dementia is completely unpredictable. Some patients regain some cognitive function, some become almost non-responsive."

"Interesting for her." whispered Claudio.

"Go tell her you love her." said Priya.

Lidia sat with her brother on the branch seat in the afternoon sun. She had been quiet until the music from a car coming to a stop hit her ears.

Before you slip into unconsciousness,
I'd like to have another kiss.
Another flashing chance at bliss,
Another kiss, another kiss.

Lidia went from slouched to bolt upright, her eyes opening in alarm as she strained to hear the words. Agitated and confused, Claudio made no connection with the song. Nicola found 'The Crystal Ship' on his phone and played it again to her as they settled her back in bed.

"Bella canzone." Beautiful song.

"Ricordi da dove?" Do you remember where?

"Da qualche parte nella mia felicitá." From somewhere inside my happiness.

Lidia fell asleep humming the opening bars until she drifted away as Nicola and Claudio held a hand each.

Claudio's face changed as he remembered.

"She hummed the song for days after she met your Father."

Claudio's mouth turned up in a smile. He remembered his sister's hopeless efforts in hiding her love for Nectarios. She concealed it well but when her brother realised, she couldn't deny her feelings. Not even he could break this bond, his sister delirious with happiness.

Nicola played it on repeat later as he ate. He loved *The Doors* and remembered the song, but now it sounded clearer, laden with nostalgia. As the flurry of cymbals and Ray Manzarek's keyboards shuddered to a close, a scratching sound came from somewhere near the front of the house. He walked through the house and listened, more scurrying and scratching. He stopped at his parents' bedroom.

He peered into the room; three black crows sat on the windowsill. Nicola left the window half a metre open in the morning for the cool change to come through. Two crows sprang at the first sound and flew out; but the third flew into the glass, panicking then tangling itself between the thin chintz curtain and the thick blinds, before freeing itself and ending up on the floor. Surveying the room, the bird flew to the highest point, on the wardrobe, emitting a loud *faarrk*. Nicola left the room watching the crow the whole way. He returned with the loaded air rifle and aimed. *Faarrk* and the *flit* of the rifle, catching the crow under its left wing as it took flight. The crow toppled forward, unbalanced and landing on the bed, before trying to fly out the window. After the third attempt, the bird lay convulsing on the floor. Nicola grabbed two old pillowcases, wrapped it up and walked outside. A short blow to the head with the butt of the air rifle put the bird out of its misery. His two companions sat on the fence as Nicola double-wrapped the pillow cased bird in thick plastic and disposed of it in the bin. He tried to wave the remaining crows away, but they ignored him and stayed. They sat on the lid of the bin for another five minutes, pecking at the edges of the lid before flying away into the night.

Nicola cleaned his parents' room, wolfed down two glasses of ice-cold water and soon found blessed sleep. At six a.m., he woke to loud banging. He opened the door and a ragged Claudio walked in.

"Cazzo. Non potevo dormire."

"I couldn't sleep either." lied Nicola.

Claudio screwed up his nose as he looked up at the ceiling. "Ma che puzza?"

Nicola smelled nothing, but Claudio's nose was acute as ever.

"A bird flew in last night."

"What kind of bird?"

"Magpie."

48

They arrived at the Austin Hospital and sat with Lidia before Dr Priya arrived.

The anaesthetist administered a mild sedative to Lidia, but the brightness of the walls still agitated her, and her feet itched. She looked around the room and reached for Nicola's arm.

"Che me fanno Nicola?" What are they doing to me?

"Just a scan, Mum." An awful white lie he had to tell to prevent all hell breaking loose.

Dr Priya took Nicola aside for the formalities as Claudio held his sister's hands. Non é l'ultima volta Claudio thought to himself. It's not the last time. He held her hand after she developed the habit of running off when they went to the shops, on the boat from Italy to ward off primed men eager for one thing, and when he gave her away to Nectarios. She had to tell him to loosen his grip as they walked down the aisle to the laughter of the nurses.

Claudio began to cry. Lidia looked at him and smiled.

"Don't be silly Claudio. Just a scan. Tell him, Nicola."

"Just a scan." said Nicola.

"I know, Lidia."

Dr Priya held Lidia's hand as she walked alongside her bed on the way to theatre.

"We're here. See you later, Mum," said Nicola as he waved to her.

"You've got lovely boys Lidia." said Priya. The anaesthetist made final adjustments and theatre staff moved busily around them.

"I love my boys."

The anaesthetist brought over his phone and as promised, played Lidia's song for her on a pair of small speakers. Jim Morrison's voice clear as Lidia sang along.

"Here we go, Lidia."

The team listened as a nurse sang along with the words as she held Lidia's hand. Manzarek's keyboard solo flowed through the room, bouncing off the white walls. The anaesthetic flowed into Lidia's vein. She felt intense heat, smelt garlic, then nothing.

Claudio and Nicola sat and made small talk to fill the void. Claudio decided not to mention Gabriella. Nicola thought about telling Claudio about Alex but found the prospect too hard. Men made small talk well until shit hit the fan.

After a tick over two hours, Priya asked for more suction
as she scanned to assess what remained. The MRI
estimated the tumour at 3 x 1 x 2cm. She was satisfied
she had removed as much as she could without causing
collateral damage. She managed to avoid Broca's area
but Priya couldn't guarantee Lidia's speech would not be
unaffected. Predicting damage to the frontal lobe was
also impossible to estimate. Her vitals were stable
throughout.

The men jumped as Priya walked through the double
doors.

"Everything went as well as can be expected."

"Is the cancer all gone?" asked Claudio.

"We hope so." she replied, before turning to scrub in for
her next surgery. She had already moved on to her next
case, a rather more problematic astrocytoma at the base
of the brainstem.

Claudio screwed his face up. "What if she wakes up and
asks for Nectarios?"

"Be happy the surgery went well."

"She forgot him overnight. What if she remembers him
overnight?"

"We deal with it."

49

Lidia lay in her bed as Nectarios came in two days after his first round of chemo. He finally had the strength to drive. He placed his hand in Lidia's as she slept, the warmth waking her. Lidia's eyes met his, warmth giving way to confusion and a shrill cry of *Aiuto! Help!* The nurse frazzled as Nectarios froze in the middle of Lidia's room until she coaxed him to leave. *Wait a couple of days* she said, *she'll come around.* After three more attempts and Lidia's distress escalating with each visit, Nicola had to convince him Lidia wasn't Lidia any longer. He went every day for a fortnight, moving from the couch outside her room to the doorway to look at her until he couldn't take it anymore. When his next chemo treatment ended, he stayed home and rang Marco every day for an update, hoping it was a bad dream.

During a further round of chemo, Nicola slept in a roll out bed for nights on end as his Father lost twelve kilos in ten weeks. Nectarios tried walking the hospital corridors, first unassisted before struggling for balance, forcing him to use a walking stick. *All this lying down is killing me* he said. Cancer hurt you the most if you stayed still, thought Nectarios. The chemo stabilised him, a false dawn. A month later the metastases gathered pace. His brain lasted well after his liver and bones were being ravaged. Nectarios chose to die at home where he felt as close as he could to Lidia, the one he remembered and loved. He lay swaddled in blankets, the way we begin life. But instead of taking his first gulp of air screaming,

Nicola expelled his last in silence. Nicola held one hand and Sia the other. Rita cried in the lounge room.

50

Gabriella looked at Claudio as he got dressed.

"I can't do this anymore."

"What do you mean?"

"What I said. You're getting too close. I was afraid you would, and it has happened."

"So why don't we see each other outside of here?"

"While I keep doing this? As if you would be Ok with me doing this if we were together. And have you forgotten? I have a boyfriend."

"So, you have imagined us together. Believe me, you would not have to do this if we were together."

"I have a boyfriend. What makes you think I would stop doing this anyway? I earn good money and look after myself. I don't need you for money. See? Dinner is never just dinner. Please don't come here again."

"Is your boyfriend Ok with you doing this. Does he even know?"

"None of your fucking business. Now get out before I call security."

"Ok, Ok. If you ever need anything," he said writing on her card, "here is my address and number."

He left the card on the bed and left. As he walked down the stairs, the man coming up bumped him hard. Claudio turned.

"Excuse me?"

At six-foot two, the man dismissed Claudio with a smirk and took a step down to meet him. They locked eyes. He leant closer to Claudio.

"Fuck off, grandpa. Did you manage to get it up?"

Claudio stunned him with a punch to the solar plexus as the man conjured up a gob to spit at him. Instead, he gagged on it and Claudio followed up with an uppercut to his undefended jaw. The man curled up small on the step beneath him, holding his face. Claudio kicked him in the balls.

"You won't need those now, will you?"

51

The courier cyclist found Kondos in his room. He asked him in a flat voice to read and sign the documents while he waited outside.

He spread the divorce settlement documents on the small table in his room and read over them. He put on the cheap magnifiers from the chemist downstairs. The house in East Hawthorn sold for $1.6M. His read his share, one-hundred and fifty thousand. His share of his entitlements brought the final figure up to just under two-hundred and fifty thousand. Legal fees, even without squabbles, ate into his share.

This is your doing, she said. He rang Olivia: *this number has been disconnected.*

He had signed the documents and called out to the courier.

In Chippendale, Sydney, Olivia walked out of the Department of Births, Deaths and Marriages. It took longer than Olivia expected to change the girls' surnames to her maiden name, Lurtacci. She rang her Mother and told her she would be home soon.

52

Nicola and Claudio sat as Dr Priya looked at the backlit scans. The lightboxes dwarfed her.

"The tumour we removed measures within five-hundred microns of what the MRI measured, half a millimetre. I managed to avoid damage to her speech area."

"Her memory?" cut in Claudio.

"Coming to that. The brain even at this age is very plastic and her memory may be erratic. Be prepared for anything."

With that, she opened the door and offered her best wishes. Nicola hugged Claudio.

"I'm off to work."

"What, where?"

"At a clinic in Brunswick. Three days a week."

"Bravo," said Claudio. "About time."

Nicola arrived at the clinic. Patients filed into the waiting room and tradesmen worked on the staff room at the back. H walked him through and met the staff. H showed his two leather chairs and a spare in the corner, and an oak desk and a lamp. He looked at his list; all but one of his seven slots booked. By his third client, he slipped into a familiar groove. He reminded himself that at its most base level, his role was to facilitate a chat to extract the issues, set an agreed course and make some recommendations. His last patient was a referral from a local psychiatrist. She cut him loose once she realised she couldn't offer him anything more than a good counsellor could.

"Hi, I'm Nicola. Please, have a seat."

"Andrei." He looked around the room. "So, Dr Tanithan divorced me."

"That implies a marriage of some kind?"

"Five years is a long time. And I'm sure your appointments, while scheduled for an hour only run for 50 minutes once the small talk's out of the way. At least with her, I got something out of the sessions."

No wonder she cut you loose thought Nicola.

By the end of the hour, Andrei outlined his stresses and anxieties in great detail. Nicola even gave him ten minutes of grace so he wouldn't have a stick to beat him with.

Nicola tidied up and sat to summarise his notes on his laptop. Then, the voice he never thought he would hear again. It was in the waiting room and he heard it among

other voices, but he was certain. He started when his
phone buzzed and shut it out as he strained to hear the
voice again. One of the receptionists poked her head in.

"Gina Liakos is here to see you, Nicola. Come and see
me later and I'll show you how to use the phone."

Nicola rushed around the room and cleaned up in a rush.
He knocked over his coffee cup and tried to catch it with
his foot, the cup catching him hard on the ankle and
coffee spilling on his shoe and floor. He rubbed it and
walked across to his door. He looked out into the waiting
area where Gina and Alex chatted. His cheek itched and
he almost drew blood scratching it and he couldn't stop
sweating. He rang reception and asked them to bring
Gina in. He sat and squirmed as he tried to look relaxed.

Gina came in, shut the door and sat on the armchair,
leaning forward and then back, unsure how Nicola would
receive her. Her darkest of brown eyes were sunken
compared to the version Nicola remembered, but that
was a month off two years ago. Her trademark black
spiralled hair sprawled out without her usual scrunchie,
and her mouth had lost its natural parabolic shape. Her
thin frame looked crumpled as she sat, hunched. She
looked a pale version of the woman he loved and yet he
sat opposite mute and captivated.

"Hi, Nicola. What song is playing in your head right
now?"

"Suedehead."

Morrissey sang in his head.

Why do you come here?
When you know it makes things hard for me?
When you know, oh, why do you come?

He stared and his vision blurred around her.

"I still have all the mixtapes you made for me, Nicola. Your cheek is bleeding."

He dabbed it with a drop of saliva and looked up at her.

"Gina, those mixtapes were from a different time. Why are you here?"

His vision cleared and he could think again as if his carotid arteries cleared after the Mother of all traffic jams.

"Dr H and Alex manage my anxiety and depression. I'm sorry for your Father." She breathed deep to try and keep herself together.

Nicola paused before replying. "So sorry that you showed the respect to not turn up to his funeral. My parents loved you."

"And I loved them Nic-"

"I loved you. How many other peoples' lives have you made cameo appearances in?"

Gina's olive face went white and she cried. "I expected you to be angry, but not an insult like that. That's a low blow. What we had was more than a cameo."

"You want insulting? How about you vanishing? No explanation, nothing. And now you find out I'm here you think I can help you with your anxieties?"

Gina pulled at loose strings of her hair, a compulsion she had overcome until now. She told herself to stop.

"I feel better seeing you Nicola. How is Lidia?"

"Dementia and as of a few days ago, brain cancer."

Gina got up to comfort him. Nicola stood, hesitated, then walked past her and opened the door.

"I can't do this Gina."

Despite Nicola's pain, Gina told herself she had turned a corner. She accepted the blows and took her small victory. She got up and looked him in the eye, placing a hand on his shoulder as she walked past. A bolt of lightning shot through Nicola's arm where she made contact. He walked back to finish his notes, dropping his pen twice.

"Is Gina OK, Nicola?" asked Alex, startling him. "She left upset. What happened?"

"Gina happened."

"Gina happened, what does that mean?"

"Join the dots, Alex."

"Oh my God."

"Oh my God what? How long has she been coming here?"

"She has been a patient here for over ten years. Right after her sister died in a car accident, she went into a deep depression and crippling anxiety. Then her Mother died of a heart attack. And then she shut down completely. She told me her relationship ended, well, she ended it, but I had no idea she meant you. How she looked after her Father for as long as she did, I don't know. She put him in a nursing home when it got too much, but he died of a heart attack too. She spent some time in hospital care. We've got her back on track bit by bit and H thought some cognitive therapy with you might help once her biochemistry was settled. She was sick of shrinks. Now what do we do?"

Nicola sat and stared into the carpet. Alex sat and saw his torment. "How did you meet her?"

"My pug, Zico was in agony, eight years old. She worked at a Vet in Clifton Hill. As soon as she held him, he settled. He knew a good soul when he met one. She looked up at me, those dark eyes and that crazy black hair trying to escape that scrunchie she wore. I fell for her in that single moment. Her hands were the last to comfort Zico as we put him out of his misery. She helped me bury him. We were together for about three years before she vanished. We never got engaged because we thought we'd go straight to marriage. I had no idea her sister or her Mother and Father died. She hid that well."

"Did you ever go to her house to find her?"

"Of course I did! But if someone doesn't want to disappear, they can, even today. Her house empty, up for sale, then sold, no auction. Her work said she left; they didn't know where she went, and she disconnected her mobile. She never got into social media and her emails bounced back. After a while, my parents' health issues took over and I gave up. I had buried that part of my life in a concrete box. Now it's blown up to pieces."

"People become damaged and fuck up every day. Today was a huge bombshell, but if you love her that much you owe her the chance to explain her side."

"By continuing her therapy?"

Alex rolled her eyes and slapped the edge of the coffee table, startling Nicola.

"Here, the Botanical Gardens, the Taj Mahal, your place, wherever. Be there. And don't punish her like an arsehole."

53

Kondos' progress exceeded Rehab staff expectations. His cognitive measures were improving as expected, but his physical strength was streets ahead of his targets. Two weeks later, his doctors and physios declared him fit to leave. He took a Taxi home, having instructed his agent in good time to have the tenants vacate his apartment in Prahran. He collected all his belongings Olivia stored in a lock up garage. He then ordered furniture online and set about cleaning the place up. He tired at around eleven p.m. and spent the night in a sleeping bag.

The next morning, he rang Rufus Stagan.

"Rufus, I'm ready to return."

He picked up on Stagan's hesitation and asked what was happening.

"Look, Savva. We had instructions from your wife. Your medical situation meant that you were unlikely to return to your role. As your medical and financial power of attorney, we had to respect her wishes-"

Olivia, you bitch. "But I'm fine now. Full rehab and I'm ready to come back."

"Professor Sanayathan stepped up after your accident and will remain in the role. I'm sure we can find a role for you somewhere in the department."

Kondos breathed in and bristled at the thought of his former student replacing him. He composed himself and continued despite the feeling of loss in his chest.

"Rufus that is my role and not yours to take from me. You made no effort to communicate with me."

"As I said, your wife-"

"You said that the FIRST TIME!"

Stagan paused before he replied in an even voice. "I won't be bullied, Savva. Either calm down and have a civilised conversation or we can cut ties now. You're on the outside looking in until I say so, remember that. I'm free tomorrow morning at eight. Don't be late."

Kondos walked the long way around to avoid the embarrassment of seeing another name on his door. *The world is against me* he said to himself. He did his best to be congenial and claw back lost ground, but Stagan was in no mood for reconciliation. He offered Kondos a minor role; three days leading dissection classes and two lectures a week, with one proviso: that he agreed to counselling to cope with his return to work. Stagan remained less than impressed with his outburst and wanted to exercise due diligence.

Kondos agreed to the terms. But far from clawing back lost ground, he was in a landslide.

54

Lidia stirred and muttered away. Pina brought in her breakfast and sat by her side until Nicola came in. After finishing her toast, Lidia cocked her head to one side and looked at him.

"Tu Papa, dov'e?"
Where is your Father?

Nicola froze, before composing himself and responding, "he'll be here one day." He practised this scenario after her operation.

"Voglio tornare a casa se non mi vuole vedere qui."
Take me home if he won't come here to see me.

She looked at Nicola's face. "La fidanzata? Dov'e'?"
And the girl you want to marry? Where is she?"

"Who?"

"Ma se non la ricordi non è giusta per te. Peccato."
If you cannot remember, she is no good for you. Shame.

She drank the last of her tea. She turned again to face him, almost looking through him to the door behind.

"Vado a riposarmi, mi sono stanco. Venga dopo con Nectario se mi vuole bene. Va."

I'm tired and I'm going to lie down. Come later with
Nectarios if he loves me. Go.

Nicola wasn't sure whether to be pleased or worried.
When he told Claudio, he showed no signs of shock. "So,
we're here."

55

Gabriella woke as the door slammed and went back to sleep. Ivan, drunk, went outside and walked around for a minute before coming back inside. He rifled through the cupboard for some home-made vodka and continued drinking outside.

Gabriella woke again at the sound of a shot glass crashing across the tiled kitchen floor, followed by Ivan cursing in Russian. Then came the footsteps down the hallway, heavy and irregular. She tried barricading herself in the bathroom, but his huge hand wrenched it open. He threw her onto the bed, her head hitting the wall before her hands could cushion the blow. He lunged at her but lost balance and fell to the floor. He grabbed her left ankle and pulled her down to him, her right leg kicking at him but only managing to scuff across the top of his bald head. He laughed at her, spit around his mouth like a bulldog.

"Stay still, *curva*. Fucking whore. Why didn't you fuck the old man in the restaurant?"

He regained his balance and stood her up, wiping spit from his mouth with his free hand and flicking it away. She tried to hold him at bay, but he held her left shoulder and arm with one hand. He smacked her across her right cheek. As she put her hand there, he slapped her hard across the left side of her neck. The pain and shock made her legs wobble and she fell to the floor. He threw her onto the bed again and climbed on top of her, yanking up her tee shirt and pulling her panties down.

"I'll give you another hole where you don't want it bitch."

Gabriella lay frozen, hoping he would collapse from the alcohol. He pulled out his cock, but dampened by alcohol, he fell on his back in a stupor, his pants halfway down. The drunken momentum of his body rolled him onto his side away from her where he settled, muttering incoherently to no one before sleep came. Objects in the dark throbbed in and out with her pulse as the pain returned. Her mouth stayed open and she breathed quietly through it, as if even that would wake him and unleash a fresh hell on her. Her neck and shoulder burned and stung from the pain coming in waves, and she was scared to move.

Her phone said 6:37 a.m. She heard Ivan's snoring and the pain subsided enough for her to move. She felt the base of the bedside lamp and wondered if it was solid enough to crush his skull. She struggled to lift her left arm above her shoulders and left it alone. She moved fast, the adrenaline focusing her attention only on those things she needed. *Fuck the rest* she thought as she slipped on her shoes and left through the back, taking care not to slip on the glass fragments and alcohol scattered over the kitchen floor. She left without bothering to close the door in case it squeaked. She drove the ten minutes home, careful not to turn her head and make the pain worse and showered. She did another brutal sweep of her own apartment as she decided what to keep. *No time for sentimentality.* She loaded her car in three trips, pushing through the pain and drove somewhere quiet for a coffee.

With an hour to go before her shift, she pulled into a parking station and walked the long way around to her work. She tried to walk into her room without anyone noticing but two women noticed her slight limp and the bruises on her face and neck.

"What the fuck?" asked one of them.

"Not now, please."

She waved the concern away, went into her room and checked the bruise. She touched the purple area larger than the size of her hand that spread from the side to the back of her neck and winced as she applied an ice pack then some Vitamin E cream. She chastised herself for letting this happen to her before reassuring herself that she had at last done the right thing. She made it through her shift and appreciated the concern two of her clients showed for her welfare. One client found the bruising arousing, forcing Gabriella to bare down and find a distant place until the arsehole finished. She left early to make sure Ivan wasn't waiting and booked herself in at a hotel in the CBD for the night, soaking in bath salts. She started looking for a new apartment, and by the next morning, she had a firmer idea on where and how she would live.

Ivan woke groggy late in the afternoon. He surveyed the bathroom. Most of her toiletries were gone. He didn't bother calling. Instead, he texted: *You'll be back*. She swiped the text away and changed her phone settings so he couldn't find her.

Nicola spent the day arranging every photo he could find of his parents into some chronological order. Lidia kept all their photos in albums by decade and Nicola marvelled at how organised she used to be. He copied them, then compiled a scrapbook to show her. He wanted to fill the gaps in her memory. He called Alex round later after work and showed her, something she appreciated.

They turned to the last page when Rita knocked on the door. Alex arrived as Rita parked her car to visit Nicola. Rita waited ten minutes before she knocked.

Nicola opened. Rita pushed the door and walked past him. "Hello, Thia?"

"Nicola, how are you? Can I come in?" she asked, already halfway down the hallway.

"Of course," he said, arms out.

Rita strode further ahead of Nicola to scrutinise the visitor. She made eye contact.

Like a young Sia. How interesting.

"I'm Rita, Nicola's auntie."

"I'm Alex, a friend of Nicola's."

"Just a friend?"

"We work together at a medical clinic."

The green eyes were pure Nectarios. When she tilted her head, Rita knew. She kept eye contact with Alex for a further second, then turned to Nicola.

"I thought I'd drop past and say hello. Aren't you going to offer me a drink?"

"What would you like?"

"A tea please, black."

Like your heart thought Nicola.

"How's Aki going in Boston?"

"He's doing very well. I don't understand that big bang stuff he is studying but he is a lecturer and enjoying himself. He met a girl."

"And Pari?"

"He is doing a construction course. Very busy."

"Construction? So, he has left real estate?"

"Yes Nicola, they are two different things."

Alex excused herself and used the bathroom. She picked up her things, mumbled thanks to Nicola for buying her time and said goodbye to Rita.

Rita smirked as she waved from her chair. "So soon, Alex? Nice to meet you. Are you Greek? Maybe you and Nicola could be more than friends one day. You would have beautiful children."

"Oh yeah. Thanks." Alex said from the hallway.

Nicola turned back as the door shut and returned to Rita's cunning smile. "What was that all about?"

"What? The more than friends? Sorry, Nicola if I embarrassed you. She looks like such a lovely girl."

She tapped her teacup slowly with her spoon.

"I know your Father had another woman after he fought with your Mother. They fought a lot after they got married. There were rumours. But a daughter? Still, Nectarios did what Nectarios wanted. And don't try and deny it. Those green eyes, the way she tilts her head. Your Father did that whenever he gave us a lecture. Why did you hide this?"

"With my Mother in her condition, I have more to worry about that keeping everyone informed."

Rita cackled. "I wonder how Claudio will react when he is 'informed'. When will you tell him? I can imagine his face. Ha!"

Nicola's face reddened and he broke out into Greek.

"I think it's time for you to leave. Dad was right."

"About what?"

"Never mind." he said, exasperated. He grabbed her cup of tea and tipped it into the sink.

Rita slapped the table. "No, no. You cannot start that and leave it unfinished. You are a big boy, explain yourself."

"Dad left me a letter to read after he died. He warned me that you would be more difficult to deal with than Sia. So far, he's right."

"Of course, Sia, always his favourite."

"Nectarios looked after you both, as brother and Father."

"You weren't there, so please don't be so righteous. What else should he have done? As the oldest, his duty was to look after us."

"And didn't you pay your respects by sitting out here while he took his last breath in his bed?"

"How dare you."

"You talked about missing out when I came to dinner that night. Missing out, days after I lost my Father. Do you not understand how twisted that is?"

"He owed us much more money than that. All that property. One hundred thousand dollars, what an insult."

"No, this is an insult. I'm asking you again to leave. Do not come here again." Nicola walked down the hallway, opened the door and waited.

"How much did he pay the *poutana* after he got her pregnant, I wonder?" said Rita as she came down the hallway. Her mouth was curled up and reminded Nicola of Bette Davis before she says *fasten your seatbelts* on the stairs in *All About Eve*.

"Please go and don't you dare talk about her like that."

"So, you've met her, have you?"

"If you have issues with your brother, go to his grave and yell at him. Do you remember where it is? Find him and get your closure that way. Maybe another hundred thousand dollars will come out of the ground like an ATM. Out!"

He pushed her through the doorway, slammed the door as she lost then regained her balance and stood by the bedroom window to make sure she left. He flopped on the bed and let his shaking body relax.

His phone rang and startled him. "Is she gone?" asked Alex.

He breathed in deep so he could talk.

"Finally. We had a full-on row. In Greek."

"You put the gloves on and got in the ring, well done."

"The number of times I've had to bite my tongue with her over the years. She's a witch, a *strigla*. Every family has one."

"She's a piece of work, that's for sure."

"I apologise for what she said, Alex. She ambushed me."

"Nah, forget it. But she had better cross the road if she sees me."

He rang Sia next.

"What took you so long?" asked Sia.

"She got to you first, didn't she?"

"Did I hear right? You went toe to toe with Rita in Greek? My compliments."

"I know, I shouldn't have-"

"She deserved it I'm sure. Don't believe half of what she says. Just ignore her. I played dumb. Petra told me about Alex anyway. She sounds lovely. When can I meet her?"

"We'll do dinner one day. Thanks for understanding."

"Don't leave it too long, Ok?"

"You're not pissed off at your brother?"

"Worse people have done better things and vice versa, Nicola. After you were born, your parents wanted a girl, but they couldn't fall pregnant again. They were distraught. When I meet her, I'll treat her like a niece."

"And again, thank you. How are you and Rita sisters?"

"She has good qualities. Just forgot where she left them."

After work the next day, Nicola and Claudio sat with Lidia over dinner and went through their history. The photos leapt out at her, and she struggled to believe the gorgeous young woman with the strawberry blonde hair was her. Nicola pointed out the small beauty spot on the right side of her neck in the photo and Lidia started crying. After a few views, they realised Lidia enjoyed playing dumb and drawing as much attention as possible. Nicola turned to the last page, their twenty-fifth wedding anniversary photo. A young Nicola sat between them. Nicola explained to his Mother that Nectarios passed away from cancer and that he didn't want her to see him suffering. She held her hand to her mouth and blew a kiss from her hand to his face. They said nothing as she processed the information. Claudio thought that in her own way, she knew all along and that the dementia made her grieving different.

Signora Calabro came into the dining area, wary of Lidia since the attack. Arthritis and a mini stroke slowed her to a shuffle. Lidia beckoned her to sit with them.

"These are my boys." said Lidia.

She coaxed her to sit next to her and showed her the book from start to end. Signor Calabro had recently passed she said, from a heart attack.

"Le mie condoglianze," said Lidia, patting her hand like an old friend, before consoling her with a hug.

Lidia asked Pina to show her the book every afternoon with a cup of tea until a week later when she asked her to put it in her valuables draw. The line between past and present filled in, Lidia was a picture of peace. Although not religious in the pious, observable sense, she prayed to be reunited with Nectarios.

"Signore, ti prego. Portami a Nectarios."
Lord, please take me to Nectarios.

Nicola walked down the street, almost tripping over himself to keep his balance. He tried to remove the note from his pocket, but it snagged, tearing the top section as he got it out. The words were intact though. Grace opened the curtains. LOOK, MUMMY, THE MAILMAN IS HERE so loud the windows vibrated into waves. Olivia opened the door and moved to him in an instant, her right hand outstretched, demanding the note. The BMW screeched and Kondos got out, his body expanding to double his height and his torso morphing into a grotesque superhero V pattern which ripped his shirt. Nicola tried to run but could only walk, the gradient too steep. Kondos stood with arms crossed in front of Nicola's car, laughing as Olivia stood behind him blocking his way back. Trapped.

Nicola woke, his chest pounding from the same dream for the third night in a row, each one more vivid than the one before, and the figures more distorted. He looked through his information and found Olivia's phone number.

58

After a succession of missed calls in either direction, Nicola answered Olivia's call.

"Olivia?"

"Who's this?"

"I'm the man who dropped you the note."

Silence, an exhalation, then her tone went up an octave.

"I was wondering when our paths would cross. I'm actually in Melbourne. Can you meet me tonight?"

"Um, sure. Is seven Ok?"

"I'll meet you out front of Readings in Lygon St. Don't worry, I'll recognise you."

Nicola flicked through the reference books and waited. Olivia showed up and waited outside, annoyed with her blonde hair coiled into a bun. She uncoiled and redid the bun without any care for whoever looked at her. Her tee and jeans looked too big for her body. Nicola thought it strange. She was attractive, tall and athletic. He took a deep breath and stepped out to meet her. She turned as he approached and shook his hand with a grip that hurt.

"Olivia Lurtacci."

"Nicola Petrakis if we're exchanging full names. Nice to meet you."

"Let's go. Follow me."

He tried to gauge her tone. Neither angry nor friendly, but not neutral either. She wasn't sure of him either. There weren't any how-to guides on meeting the person who outs your husband as a rapist.

She walked without a word into University Cafe and demanded the quietest table at the back. The waiter moved the reserved sign to another table. Nicola wavered, still assessing her.

"We can sit down and check each other out if you want. We're going to be here a while and if I can impose, I'll be staying at your place tonight. We've got a lot to talk about. I moved my flight to ten-thirty in the morning. Oh sorry, how presumptuous of me. Do you live alone?"

"Yes." His cheek went again.

"Just for my curiosity, how did you get my number?"

"I used to work for Victoria Police."

They ordered a pasta and a red wine each.

Olivia looked up. "So, why did you call me? And please, relax."

"I better start from the beginning. Your husband-"

"Ex-husband."

" - raped my cousin."

"What is her name?"

"Excuse me?"

She pulled out a USB.

"Three days after the accident, I cleared his office and found these in the bottom of his filing cabinet - seventeen of them. He had a camera concealed within a hollowed-out textbook on the shelf. Each USB had a rape recorded on it, so I'm familiar with the names. Which one was she?" Her voice softened and she began to tear up.

"Petra Rouveliotis." he said, watching for her reaction.

She let out an abrupt high-pitched cry that raised diners' heads from their tables, before getting up and hugging Nicola. "I'm so sorry this happened to her, Nicola." He put his arm around her, careful not to be too firm.

"She fought him off, kicked him and got away. I watched it."

"When she told me, I called and confronted him. He was cocky but denied it."

"I bet. Go on."

"Then," he hesitated, "I did the stupid thing I did. I had no idea he was off, had no idea Grace would confuse me with the mailman. It got out of hand and the chase and the crash. And here we are."

"How could you know he was off that day? Hang on, how do you know my daughter's name?

"I worked at Victoria Police; it was easy to find out. I was going to call the police. Then I had a dream about a friend who was raped at Uni. It shook me, and I took a different course. I wanted to punish him. And here we are. In hindsight, I should have called you, but I thought seeing the words would make you believe it. I felt bad for you."

"I wished you had called the police, or the medical faculty itself where he did these things."

Nicola shrugged and leaned in closer to Olivia, pointing to the USB in her bag. "Sorry, but why haven't you handed these into the cops?"

"I want to protect my daughters. I don't want to stain Maya and Grace. I divorced him and used the USBs as a threat to make sure I got what was mine and that he wouldn't come near us. They're too young. They think he had an affair. Pathetic isn't it?"

"Well, it's done, and we are where we are. If you don't hand the USBs in, how does he face the music for what he has done? Me going to the police based on my cousin's accusation is one thing. He could have hidden the USBs and the camera if he got wind of anything and dragged out any proceedings. Now, there is tangible proof."

"Are you moralising me?"

"Neither of us can leave things as they stand. And if the police knew you held onto this without turning him in, how would they view that, dimly, no?"

She nodded in resignation.

"You're right. Can you give me some time to sort our lives out? We've moved to Sydney and there's lots to do. I don't want him to find us."

Nicola accepted that this was as much as he was going to get and agreed.

"How far is your place?" she asked.

"We can walk. Fifteen minutes."

On the way back, they tried to talk about anything except Kondos. Nicola offered to carry her backpack, but she refused. In the end, they settled on silence until the rain almost caught them short. Nicola made her a bed, gave her a towel and put on some coffee. Olivia looked around the kitchen and asked him about his parents. She was a good listener and empathised with Nicola's great sadness as he recounted their stories.

"Look, it has been a heavy night. I'm off to bed. Let me know if you need anything." said Nicola.

"Me too. Thank you, Nicola. Goodnight."

He settled himself and found sleep. The click of his bedside lamp woke him an hour later. He turned and saw Olivia in bra and panties, light and shadow defining her breasts, obliques, calves and the lips above the dark of her neck. He took it all in and shunned the uproar in his mind. She climbed on top of him. Nicola put one of his hands on her face and the other on her left breast.

"Not a fucking word." she whispered, as she rubbed herself against him. He pulled her down and kissed her, her hair engulfing his face. He inhaled deeply and took in her smell. She rubbed herself hard and lowered herself slow.

"I need this." she said in a guttural voice and rode him at a gentle pace, holding his hands against the wall and dictating the rhythm, towering over him like a Goddess he was helpless to defy. She stared through him, burning a hole in his brain, clamping him before the sum of her muscular contractions converged on him. She slowed and then picked up the pace again, urging him to come. He almost blacked out as his sweet release came.

Olivia lent down and whispered into his ear. "The great thing about men is that they only have enough blood supply to run either their brain or their dick at any one time."

They lay motionless for minutes.

"You stole that from Robin Williams." he said, laughing.

"Doesn't make it less true. Thanks for not thinking, you were great."

"You're amazing."

"I know." She winked.

Nicola hit her arse hard with his pillow. "Modest, aren't we?"

They laughed some more then fell asleep a foot apart. She wanted her space again. Nicola stared at the ceiling and wondered what was next. They woke and showered apart, saying nothing until they were driving to the airport. She bought Nicola breakfast before getting up at the first boarding call.

She kissed his cheek. "Thanks for last night. I'll be in touch about the other thing." she said, pursing her lips. Nicola would have killed for her at that moment. As he sat in the car, he could still smell her. He looked around. Her scarf lay on the back seat. He held it to his face and breathed it in.

After inhaling the smell of the scarf every day for a week, he put it in a large zip lock bag in the laundry cupboard. The same perfume that drove him crazy now did nothing for him. The spell broken, he exhaled and made a mental note to call Olivia and get her address.

59

Kondos sat opposite Stagan for their agreed review. He had seen the faculty counsellor three times. What she had to say didn't impress Stagan, though he couldn't let on. Although a pragmatist, Stagan wasn't sure he was about to do the right thing.

"How are things?" Stagan asked.

"If you mean regurgitating basic anatomy well below my station and standing, earning half my previous salary, then great."

"Look. it can't be easy." He paused. He wondered if he was doing the right thing but pressed on. "A colleague of mine in Sydney is retiring. Can't say which University but he's the Head of the Anatomy Department there. He asked me for a recommendation, and I offered your name as a candidate. You still need to interview but my word carries a great deal of weight with their choice."

Kondos looked at Stagan and concluded from his expression that he was keen to be rid of him. The feeling was mutual, but he maintained the congenial patter.

"I'm interested, Rufus. Thank you for your kind recommendation"

"Very well. I'll inform him and pass on your details."

Kondos shook his hand and strode off, his steps longer and more relaxed. He looked forward to the new opportunity ahead to recoup his academic standing and put the past behind. He concluded that he had paid dearly for his behaviour, both physically and professionally, even though he considered the student interactions as fair trades. He flew to Sydney and impressed Professor Ian Raleigh with his academic contributions that were remarkable for a man so young. Recruiting outside of Sydney would ruffle feathers, and the role was a good four months away. Some back and forth managing the succession was inevitable, but he would soon find out. *It would be an honour to follow in your footsteps, Professor Raleigh,* Kondos said with all the humility he could fashion. He approached the next week's lectures with renewed enthusiasm. He even showed tolerance to students having difficulty with basic concepts.

Rumours in the faculty travelled fast, actual news even faster. Petra overheard students on the first day back talking about Kondos' imminent move. She clenched her teeth so hard she didn't realise she had drawn blood from the side of her tongue.

60

The text woke Nicola early the next morning.

The prick is taking a role in Sydney.

She picked up before it had a chance to ring.

"He's taking a departmental head role in Sydney."

"That's not good." He processed the implications for Olivia and the girls. "How long?"

"No idea."

"Leave it to me." he said.

"Don't do anything stupid this time, Nicola."

"Duly warned."

He soon learned he was due to start in four weeks from a few calls to Sydney University. He had planned to call Olivia after patients, but she got to him first.

"I left something in your car." He heard her voice and was relieved it had no effect on him. "Not keeping a trophy, are we?"

"Guilty of laziness Olivia, sorry." He heard a male voice in the background.

She moved to another room and spoke softer. "Look I didn't just ring about the scarf. I wanted to be upfront. I've met someone. I think we're a blended family. He has an eleven-year-old boy.

"That was quick."

"We met a few weeks ago. He's an endocrinologist I met through a friend. We clicked straight away."

"I'm very happy for you Olivia. Does this lucky man have a name?" He heard voices and chaos in the background.

"Ben. Look, we're running late for a school thing. I'll text you my address for the scarf. Bye-"

He texted her the next morning. Need to talk ASAP.

He rang her just before midnight. Olivia answered with an angry whisper.

"It's been a long day and I'm not a night owl. What is it?"

"Savva." Silence.

"What about him?"

"He's taking a role in Sydney as Head of Anatomy."

"What? Are you sure?" She strained hard to keep her voice calm.

"I verified it - he starts in three weeks. Time to come clean with Ben and send in the USBs."

"Oh no. I made a deal with him to not come near us. I can't tell Ben this, we've only just settled into family life."

"Yes, and the USBs were your deterrent. But now that you're settled, why run the risk? And why base your relationship with Ben on a lie in case he gets cold feet?"

"Look this is a lot right now."

"It's a lot at any time if you look at the circumstances. And by the way, have you changed your phone number, Apple ID, so he can't find you?"

"Yes."

"I'll call you tomorrow."

61

Olivia looked at her bedside clock: 2.14 a.m. She swung herself onto the floor and made a cup of tea, stubbing her toe in the process. Ben shuffled in and rubbed his eyes.

"Come on, what is it?"

"What?"

"What do you mean what? You've been tossing all night."

Get it out, you fucking idiot. "It's my ex-husband."

"He tried to contact you?"

"I left him because we had grown apart, that's true, and we came back to Sydney to start fresh, which is also true, but, there's more to it."

"Ok then, it's obviously difficult but you've come this far, so just tell me. How bad could it be?"

She could only meet his eyes for a second. "That bad?" he asked.

"Ok, promise me you'll let me finish. This has been killing me." She sipped her tea and took in a deep breath. "It was a few months ago. He had a day off. It was raining. A man turned up and dropped a note into my letterbox and walked back to his car. Grace thought he was the postie and ran out. I grabbed the note, Savva arrived back from the shops and I read the note. He knew from my face."

"I don't understand. He knew what? What did the note say?"

"That Savva had been raping students in return for pass grades."

"What?!"

"Shh… he saw my expression and chased the man in his car. I got the next-door neighbour to watch the girls and I followed him. Savva crashed into a tram and was badly injured."

"I cleaned out his office and found USB sticks and a camera hidden in a textbook. He recorded each rape. I took them and decided to take the girls with me and force a divorce on my terms."

"What do you mean on your terms?"

"I used the USBs as a threat if he tried to dispute the terms or come look for us."

"But you handed them into the police, right?" He saw her expression and his face reddened.

"You still have them, don't you?"

She nodded. "In a bank safety deposit box."

Ben walked around to her side of the dining table, sat down and turned her chair to face his so they were squared up to each other. "That you didn't tell me this till now, that upsets me, but we'll come back to that. How can someone of any conscience not turn these things in so this creature can never do it again? How do you know he hasn't? How do these poor girls feel knowing he's still enjoying his freedom?"

"I used them as a deterrent-"

"Yes, I heard that the first time. But once you were up here, away from him, you should have turned them over. Each of these crimes, the anguish, the fear and the terror these girls went through. You're a competent and smart woman, but you got this wrong, very wrong, Olivia."

"I was going to, but then we met and I thought you wouldn't-"

"I wouldn't what, stay with you because of something you had no part in, no responsibility for?"

"He's moving to Sydney. He accepted a role as Head of Anatomy up here. He moves here in two weeks. The guy who dropped the note off rang me and told me. He also said I should hand them in."

"Which is what you're going to do. You're going to post these to the Medical Faculty, anonymously of course, and strongly advise them to hand them over to the police or you will. We're doing it straight after drop offs."

"We?"

"Yes, we. We need this to clean our slate. I can't have this hanging over your head any longer. Is there anything else I should know?"

"Just that I love you, Ben."

"And I love you," he said. "Now let's get some sleep."

He held Olivia until her muscles relaxed and sleep found her. He stared at the ceiling and then looked across at her again. The space was empty for three years. When breast cancer finally claimed Adelina, he expected the cold to accompany him to his grave. But now, complicated was preferable to loneliness.

Once it was done, she rang Nicola.

"He knows everything."

"I'm sorry Olivia-"

"No, no, that's just it, he absorbed it all. I copped the Mother of all serves from him, but he still loves me. He's so calm, Nicola. I couldn't believe it. He lost his wife to breast cancer three years ago. I was the first woman he had dated since. He was sure. And now, so am I."

"Ok, that's one hurdle you can tick off. A big happy family. Do the kids get along?"

"Poor Jeremy had no idea what hit him, but they love each other. Ben and I sent the USBs to the medical faculty head that I spoke to after the accident. Anonymous, of course. I included a note telling them to pass these on to the police or be embarrassed. Let justice flow from there. I kept copies in a bank safety deposit box as a plan B. I'll destroy them once he's arrested."

Go Ben. thought Nicola.

She sucked in a deep breath and thanked him.

"When he climbed up the ladder, I was proud of him. He was so doting on Grace and Maya. Then he lost focus of us. He videotaped these awful acts and he never took videos of his own daughters."

"Well now you have a new family to replace all that with. Move on, Olivia. I'm very happy for you."

"Thank you."

"Nicola, about that night."

"Locked in a vault, Olivia. Don't stress."

"I know that. I was going to say thank you. You've changed my life."

Ivan watched Gabriella walk to her car after her shift. He followed her to her new apartment in Flemington. Crossing the road, he almost got bowled over by a tram before watching her enter the block. She looked back from the first-floor landing to see him walking back to his car. She called in the favour she never thought she would need.

She insisted on meeting Claudio on neutral ground first. He wondered why they had to meet in Yarraville but was happy to see her. She gave him a tentative embrace and she winced at the light pressure on her neck. The bruise had faded but it was still very sore. He touched the area and winced in sympathy.

"Who did this? Who are you running from?"

"Ivan. I don't feel safe with him anymore. When he did this, I had to get away."

"Why stay with him? He's not a man. He doesn't deserve to breathe the same air you breathe!" Claudio's face reddened.

"Hey, hey, calm down. I *am* away from him now. I moved from my apartment in North Fitzroy to Flemington. Problem is, he followed me home and watched me walk in. Then he left."

"Do you want to stay with me?"

"Could I?" Relief as she didn't to ask herself.

"It will be my honour to keep you safe from that bastard. Let's eat and we'll move your things."

They enjoyed the sun and headed back to her apartment to collect her things. They managed to move everything in one trip between their two cars. He made up the queen size bed he had kept in his spare room for visitors. He insisted she park in his garage off the rear laneway. He fussed over her to make sure she was comfortable, showed her around the house and gave her a key. Far from obsessive, Gabriella found him a gentleman whose generosity overwhelmed her. He had no agenda. She was relieved and safe, two things she hadn't been for a long time.

63

Gabriella slept well. She woke to the aroma of Claudio's espresso and scrambled eggs with chopped basil and tomatoes.

"Eat. I'm going to see my sister." He explained Lidia's predicament and told her to make the house her own.

Lidia looked thinner and paler when he and Nicola arrived. Pina was apologetic as she told them both that Lidia lost another five kilos in ten days. She refused to eat.

"She even told us to make her spaghetti with oil and garlic. Then she smelt it and sent it back."

"I will not eat!" Lidia roared, her voice with more bass than normal, booming across the room. "I want my body to eat itself until there is nothing left. My time is up, UP, DO YOU HEAR ME?!"

Nicola and Claudio were helpless in calming her and didn't argue when she asked them to leave. They sat opposite Del Vecchio.

"She's losing too much weight. Her mind and body are running on fumes. We took some blood and booked in imaging for tomorrow. Can you bring that *Doors* song she loves?"

"Of course."

"Tomorrow at ten."

Outside, Claudio felt sick and slammed his fist into his chest, punishing himself for not being there. Nicola too felt side-tracked, but he grabbed Claudio by his arms and led him to the oak bench to calm down. They sat in silence until Claudio spoke.

"Di guerra, caccia e amuri, per un gusta milli duluri."

"In war, hunting and love, a thousand cuts for one pleasure," said Nicola.

"If we knew at eighteen what joy and pain we would experience in the next forty, fifty years, would we want it?" asked Claudio.

"Is there a choice?"

"And again, I say; I should be dying, not her." He got up, kissed his nephew on the forehead and drove away.

Claudio walked in to find Gabriella making dinner. He took in the aroma of basil and garlic that filled the house. She combined the basil and prosciutto into the al dente risotto.

She looked at him. "Lidia?"

"Yes," he nodded, "More weight loss, more tests."

Gabriella stopped cooking and hugged him. *"Coraggio,* Claudio."

"Ok," he said to her. "What delizia have you prepared?"

"Risotto, Sicilian style."

He murmured mmm in appreciation as he took his first mouthful.

"Even if you didn't cook, you would be a treasure for any man, but this-"

The knock on the door cannoned down the hallway. He walked on his socks to his bedroom and looked from the window.

"Open the fucking door!"

Claudio walked back to the kitchen and motioned to Gabriella to go into the laundry and stay quiet. He returned to the door and asked who it was.

"Her boyfriend, old man. Don't make me break your door down and hurt you."

"Good luck," Claudio said. The door was thick and heavy jarrah. The first and only thud confirmed it. Ivan groaned as he walked to his car, holding his shoulder. From the window, Claudio saw Ivan made the cut-throat sign to him. He screeched as he drove away.

Claudio went to the garage looked at her car. *È
impossibile*. He ran his hand under the wheel arches and
found what he was looking for under the front right - a
small magnetic box which Ivan used to track her. It fit in
the palm of his hand. He moved the switch to off and put
it in his pocket.

Nicola knocked on Claudio's door. *Cazzo* thought Claudio. He swallowed and let him in. He introduced Gabriella as she walked into the kitchen.

"Hi, I'm Nicola. Claudio's nephew."

"I'm Gabriella, I'm a friend of your uncle's." She opened her eyes wider for Claudio to explain. He started and stuttered before Gabriella rolled her eyes.

"Save it, Claudio. In a nutshell, your uncle used to visit me for sex. I'm a sex worker. My half Russian, half Romanian boyfriend with anger issues went too far and hit me. I left him but he is a jealous, obsessive bastard who won't leave me alone. Your uncle kindly took me in. He's a sweet man."

"Yes, he is." Nicola wasn't bothered in the slightest about the circumstances. He was still fixated on how much she resembled Morena.

"I do look like her don't I, Nicola? Don't worry Claudio, I saw your shrine to Morena. She was a beautiful, beautiful woman. Far more beautiful than me."

Nicola didn't see this blowing over, but Lidia came first. "We better go."

"Good luck for Lidia." said Gabriella.

They arrived a few minutes late but in time for Nicola to connect his phone to the MRI speakers. Lidia hummed along and her fidgeting stopped, her body relaxing as the machine whirred around her head. They walked with her as her bed rolled back to her room.

"*Ho fatto bene*, Nicola?"

"You did very well, Mum."

Del Vecchio looked at the blood test results while he waited for the images. No markers, but elevated platelets. From this, he concluded that there was no organ affected beyond the brain. Primary brain tumours rarely metastasised beyond the brain or spinal cord. He opened the attachment and the images unfolded across his three screens. He saw it and closed his eyes and looked again to be sure. The growth snaked its way along the left central sulcus, and far from the regular and defined appearance of the first growth, this one spread in a ragged pattern. It was at least double the size of the one removed from the frontal lobe and invaded her taste area, explaining her lack of appetite. Her hearing would be the next to go, then vision, speech and beyond. As the border between the cerebral and the frontal cortex, the tumour cut off her thinking from her emotional control, her language, memory, her judgement, her everything. It was inoperable and Del Vecchio hoped Lidia would not die a

slow, painful death. He called Frantz and made time to
see Nicola and Claudio the next morning.

From the faces of Frantz and Del Vecchio, they knew the
news wasn't good.

Frantz began. "The cancer has spread to another part of
her brain." He let them take that in,

"Can we do another operation?" asked Claudio.

"I'm sorry Claudio. This one is inoperable. It is larger
and difficult to remove without causing more damage.
Risk of stroke, her current status. Chemotherapy would
be fatal. Histology suggests the cells are grade three -
dividing, so this one is far more aggressive. I'm sorry."

"How long does she have?" asked Claudio, his voice
shaking.

"I'd say within three months."

After a sharp intake of breath, Claudio collapsed and
grabbed his upper left chest. Del Vecchio rang the
ambulance while Frantz commenced CPR. Minutes later,
Nicola was riding in the back with him.

"You can't go before your sister." he pleaded.

At the Austin, they stopped Nicola at the second door
and forced him to sit in the now heaving waiting room,
where eyes watched him in his agitated state. He called

work to cancel his afternoon bookings and sat in a quiet
corner of the cafeteria.

Four floors up, Dr Yin Chang nodded with satisfaction at
the stent. The 3D image showed good alignment and
blood was flowing well.

"There we go Claudio, patent again." he said, satisfied.

Nicola became irritated at the lunchtime rush. He took
the lift up to the cardiac ward and rested in the quiet of a
waiting area with a long fake leather couch. Two and a
half hours later, his phone beeped.

"Your uncle is asking for you."

Dr Chang explained with great authority the occlusion
and his stent.

"Few people survive ninety per cent occlusion. He is a
very lucky man."

Claudio stirred at the sound of Nicola's footsteps then
dozed off again. He woke later and stared at Nicola.

"I heard you in the ambulance, Nicola. Then I see this
cloud, then Morena."

"What was she doing?"

He made a beckoning gesture, barely able to lift his hand off the sheets. "Come to me Claudio, come. But I said not yet."

"You had a ninety percent blockage in your coronary artery."

"Not my turn Nicola, not my turn. There is still work to do."

The nurse shooed Nicola after five minutes, a burly woman with spiked hair. Time made the tattoo on her right forearm indecipherable and distorted.

"Don't think about bringing any relatives in tonight, Ok? I get it, you're Italian, but the man needs his bloody rest."

Nicola drove past his house to see Gabriella. She was cooking again, Nicola saw the arancini and remembered Lidia. "Gabriella, Claudio's in hospital."

"What?!"

"We found out this morning that Lidia's cancer has spread, and he fell on the spot; a heart attack They put a stent in. He is a lucky man."

"Take me to him, please. And your poor Mother. Are you Ok, Nicola?"

"No, no. He needs rest. They kicked me out. Mum is in a bad way. I'm just fucking tired of all this, this sickness." He cried again.

Gabriella hugged Nicola and sat him down. "Here, eat." she said, plating up some arancini she made with the leftover risotto. She rubbed his back as he ate.

Nicola ate and nodded in appreciation. "Who taught you to cook? My Mother's aren't as good as these."

"Wash your fucking mouth out. You're talking about your Mother. The old wogs knew how to cook."

"No, these are that good. You should be in a restaurant."

They sat and ate some more. "You're odd." she said.

"How so?"

"I tell you I'm a sex worker and you don't show any judgement, not even a silent one. I can tell when people are judging. I've always been able to read people."

"Seems like our jobs overlap quite a bit." he said before adding, "psychologist."

She laughed and snorted.

"Love a woman who snorts when she laughs."

Gabriella poured some wine for them both.

"Tell me about the love of your life, Nicola."

"How do you know I've met her?"

"Oh please - you've got bruised written all over you."

"Ok. Gina was my first serious girlfriend. We got very serious, met each other's parents, looked at houses."

"So, what happened?"

"She vanished. She changed her mobile number, left her parent's house, then sold it. I didn't see or hear from her for two years. And then two weeks ago she turns up at the clinic I work at."

"How did she look?"

"Like someone who just went through hell, a lot of hell. I later found out she lost her sister; her Mother and her Father went into a nursing home. She went into a deep depression."

"So, you tried to find a reason and listened. That takes courage."

Nicola bowed his head.

"Not exactly. In fact, not at all. I was angry at her, let her have it and asked her to leave. I found out all that other stuff later from her GP." Nicola blushed in embarrassment.

She glared at him.

"Now who's judging?" Nicola said.

"So, the first time you see her in over two years, and you punish her? The fuck is wrong with you? Be angry but find out why. She made an effort."

He looked at Gabriella and said, "I know, you're right."

"So? I presume you can contact her from details at the clinic? Arrange another 'appointment'. Christ, sometimes you men are simply not worth it."

66

Nicola sat Alex down in his room.

"I need you to make another appointment for Gina."

"Why don't you make it with her? You ended it."

"I was a dick, I admit it. If you talk to her, she may come back."

"I'll try but I don't like your chances. How's Lidia?"

"Her brain cancer has spread to the other side. Inoperable. Three months."

Alex consoled him until her next patient arrived. Nicola felt worn down but took a deep breath and began his clients. His last was Sario Florinos, fifty-seven. He lost his wife six months earlier. H convinced him to see Nicola. After losing over twenty kilos, his clothes were far too big for him. With his wife gone, he had no appetite to shop for clothes without her. His thin six-foot frame shrunk with excessive spinal curvature. He had a shaven bald head and a goatee speckled bright white with black hairs as a taunt. He sat, eyeballed Nicola and said *this life is shit but it's the one we've got*, before placing a small foldable chess board on the table next to him.

"Can't disagree." said Nicola, watching the chess board.

"Do you play chess, Nicola?"

"Used to."

"Life's like chess and it isn't. The opening is crucial, you must develop your pawns and knights. But beyond that tenet, chess is at the same time awfully dogmatic yet without rules. You start well, anything is possible."

"I'm happy to talk about chess, but what about why you're here?"

"I'm not talking about chess. I'm using it as a metaphor for life. When I say anything is possible, I mean good and bad. For me, whether I win or lose isn't important. I have won and lost. The important thing is to show up, again and again. You get skewered or forked, you must move on."

"You said life is shit but it's the only one we've got. What makes you say that?"

"About five years ago, Thanassis Veggos, the actor passed away."

"I grew up on him."

"Well, my uncle was telling my Father that 'O *Veggos psofise*'. My Father berated him and said '*no, O Veggos pethane*', and that *psofise* was for animals, not humans. My uncle said we are all animals, so what is the difference? They had an almighty row over it."

"I've always found it interesting that the Greek language had different words for animals dying versus humans dying. Who is right?"

"They didn't know it, but they both were. They have both passed, but they're probably still arguing somewhere. We are animals that possess overarching physical, emotional and intellectual capacities that make us human. We veer from one to the other. In all his movies, Veggos pushes on, with everything stacked against him with that smile and humour that made him human to us. Somewhere in that muddy explanation is why I am still here. We have to move on."

Nicola listened to how Florinos and his wife met, their raising of three boys who spread their wings to all corners of the earth, before a routine medical procedure took his wife without warning.

"It was supposed to be a routine colonoscopy," said Florinos. "She had a reaction to the anaesthesia, and It went pear shaped from there. She died of respiratory failure on the table. I'm only here because H pestered me until I said yes. I'm sure you're good at what you do, but I'm stuck on any given day between any of the five stages of grief."

"Which one are you feeling right now?"

"I'm lurching from depression into any of the other four. Today, probably bargaining. For me, these 'stages' are not a linear process. She was everything, my Irene."

"I'm not offering miracles, Sario. Talking helps. I've just lost my Father and my Mother has a clock running down on her. Cancer, inoperable. Bargaining, talking to other people. It can help."

"And no one really knows what you're going through unless they've been going through it."

"Keep coming, Sario. We can help each other. I'll try not to indulge myself too often."

They discussed Sario's daily routine and occasional work as a lawyer. He exercised daily and ate well. He thanked Nicola and offered him a game of chess. Nicola declined.

67

By ten a.m., Liana Trigo, already distracted with
unnecessary issues, opened the mail later than normal.
As the faculty office manager, she handled the incoming
mail with pragmatic cool, but the mountain of
correspondence looked daunting, even for her. She
started with the yellow express post satchels. Second
from the bottom was a padded yellow package marked
URGENT AND CONFIDENTIAL She put it on Stagan's
desk before returning to attack the rest.

The package caught Stagan's eye. He turned it over. The
sender was an Anon in North Ryde. He opened it up and
handled the hollowed-out text, camera inside and lens
poking through the spine. He narrowed his eyes at the
small individual zip lock bags, each with a single USB.
A surname on the white panel done with a labelling
machine. He read the note, typed in Times New Roman:

Att: Stagan
Hand these over to the police for everyone's good.
I'd hate for you and the faculty to be embarrassed if they
weren't.
Anon

He shut the door and inserted a USB titled SOLANGE.
Stagan advanced the video. Kondos was talking to a
female student. He advanced it further. Kondos
approached her, her posture looking defeated. She
stripped in front of him, before he lay her on her back

and forced himself inside her. Her hands covered her eyes as he raped her for fifteen minutes. He came over her body and told her she had earned her pass. Stagan looked around to be sure no one was watching although his door was locked, and his window was high on the fifth floor. He counted seventeen USBs, seventeen students and pain for all involved. He emailed all members of the faculty board and scheduled a meeting for the next morning and rang Victoria Police, asking for sex crimes. He was immediately put through to Detective Nat Rawson and explained what he knew. She met him an hour later and commended him for his honesty as he handed over the USBs and camera.

"I'll note that as head of the faculty, you were upfront and transparent."

"When will you arrest him? He's due to leave for his new role in a matter of days."

"Leave that to us. You've done your duty. We'll be in touch to obtain details of the women he raped, presumably all students here."

"Yes. I'm quite shaken up by this."

"With all due respect Professor, some perspective please. Try the women in these videos."

"I don't want to sound protective, but I hope the faculty won't be implicated."

"If you mean implicated in a criminal sense, no. If you mean by reputation and association, I can't prevent that. Once it's news and a court case commences, all bets are off. After all, Kondos raped these women, not you - Ok?"

Stagan chided himself at his selfishness for asking the question. He apologised to the detective and saw her out.

Kondos walked out of the estate agent's office. He was happy to drop the rent by ten dollars a week and leave the furniture in the apartment for the security of a two-year lease. He drove home and began packing. He found an apartment in Glebe within walking distance to the University. At two am he called it a night. He was ready. He woke to a persistent knock on the door around seven. He opened the door to three policemen behind two detectives.

"Good morning, Mr Kondos. Detective Nat Rawson, Detective Luke Monzon. May we come in?"

"What's this about?" *The bitch handed me in.* He stood his ground in the doorway.

"We need you to come with us. Come quietly?"

Kondos saw the equation, smiled and turned to show his hands.

"Savvas Kondos, you're under arrest for rape and sexual assault."
An hour later, he sat opposite Rawson and Monzon.

"Are you comfortable?"

"Yes."

"Savvas Kondos, respected academic and former head of anatomy. Let's start."

"Professor Kondos to you."

"Excuse me?"

"Professor Kondos. I would appreciate it if you would use my proper title."

"Mister's as high as it goes here," said Rawson flatly. "We have good reason to believe that you raped seventeen women over a two-year period. Students at your university."

Silence. Rawson continued.

"Seventeen, that's quite a run. How would you get away with it? Move to Sydney, climb to the top of that ladder without anything ever surfacing?"

"I am about to commence a vital role up there. This is pretty inconvenient. Can I call my lawyer, please? No further comment without her."

Sally Weekes conferred with Kondos and then sat. "You claim seventeen allegations of rape against Dr Kondos. Any proof?"

Rawson turned to her partner. "Monzon?"

Monzon returned with a shoebox. He placed it on the table and lifted the lid. Rawson lifted the zip lock bag. Weekes saw her client go pale and slump as the USBs jangled with Rawson's gentle shaking of the bag.

"Recognise these, Professor?"

Monzon held up the hollowed text and opened it to reveal the camera and lens. "I'm no anatomy student, but I doubt that Moore & Dalley would approve of you using their text as a clandestine recording device."

Weekes asked to speak with her client.

"Take all the time you need." said Rawson as she and Monzon left the room.

Weekes turned to Kondos. "What the fuck have you gone and done?"

He stared at the table, hands crossed and mute.

"Plead guilty and you may receive a reduced sentence; best scenario." She tore out a scrap of paper and scribbled. "Here are a couple of criminal defence lawyers. This is out of my league and comfort zone." "He'll be making alternative legal arrangements," said Weekes as she walked past Rawson and Monzon. Rawson asked the officers to come into the room with her.

"Mr Kondos, we'll be holding you in custody until we can arrange a hearing tomorrow morning."

68

Olivia's phone rang as they started dinner. She listened as Rawson outlined the charges against her husband.

"He is my ex-husband. We got divorced three months ago."

"Did you know, I mean that he could be capable of this?"

"No. I'm shocked, but then he was a stranger for the last two years of our marriage, always distant and consumed by his work. Now if you don't mind, we're having dinner."

"Of course. It was just a courtesy call. Thanks, Olivia."

She looked at Ben and nodded. Maya threw a potato at Jeremy and life returned to normal for her. She smiled and relished the minutiae of family life and sibling rivalries to come. Ben squeezed her arm and kissed her on the head. After dinner, he brought out a cheat's tiramisu he had whipped up that afternoon. He served Olivia her piece.

Jeremy said, "Take your time and savour it.".

She dug her spoon in and felt a metal clan against the glass bowl. Jeremy nudged Maya. She tapped it again and looked at Ben. *Poker face*, Ben said to himself. She grabbed another spoon and divided the piece and whooped with delight. She ran with the ring to wash off the mascarpone and put it on.

"It's perfect Ben. I do!" She jumped into his arms and squeezed him tight.

Maya and Grace ran around to Jeremy and hugged him so tight he almost choked.

"Does this mean Jeremy is our brother?" asked Grace and Maya.

"Yes, silly billy." said Jeremy as he tickled them both.

Olivia texted Nicola before she drifted off to sleep.

Nicola read it and smiled.

He's in custody...and I'm engaged!

The next day, Kondos pled guilty to all counts of rape and didn't request bail. He saw no sense in expensive legal posturing and threw away the names Sally Weekes gave him. The judge ordered sentencing in six weeks to allow for victim impact statements. She also ordered a psychological evaluation.

69

Petra read the letter and re-read it.

She texted Nicola:

Kondos in custody - pleaded guilty.

I know. Good.

Going to do a victim impact statement.

Tell me when so I can come and support you.

This wouldn't have happened if not for you.

Does your Mum know?

She knew something was wrong. I told her. Mothers always know.

She responded that she would be willing to provide a Victim Impact Statement in court. She put aside her pathology notes and began drafting.

Nine of the seventeen victims either did not respond or responded that they would not attend. Three would attend but not provide a statement. Five had accepted the opportunity to provide one.

Nicola's crows were back, two sitting on the roof above his parents' bedroom window. He shooed them as he got home from seeing Lidia. It was a good day, Lidia eating at last, but she fatigued during conversation, and fell asleep as her food settled. He changed and went to see Claudio. He looked surly, managing to rub the wrong way each nurse who looked after him. If it wasn't the two hourly observations, it was the order to stay in bed.

"He has been very trying, your uncle." said a nurse called Rosarita in a deep Filipino accent.

"I want to go so I can stop bothering you." snapped Claudio.

"Relax Mr Claudio, please. You are going nowhere until your cardiologist says you can go."

"I feel fine, *cazzo*. Nicola, leave me and go see your Mother."

"I was there this morning for breakfast and lunch."

"Now go for dinner. How many more times will she be able to recognise you? Go."

Nicola left Claudio be with his frustration and took his advice. He bought some ricotta cannoli in.

"Ah Nicola, you are back again?"

"I brought some ricotta cannoli."

"Lovely. We eat these after dinner," she winked. They ate together and Nicola felt awful that he hadn't spent more time there. He retained clear memories from an earlier age than most. His parents wondered how he knew things that happened when he was only four or five. He remembered his Mother as the young, energetic woman who raised him, who cooked then worked when Nicola started school. He saw the division of labour between his parents and wondered how they kept it all together. Modern couples fractured over petty issues but these two were an impenetrable unit. He then thought of Rena and Alex and their resilience in tougher circumstances. But the toughest crumble to their smallest parts, he thought. He looked up at his Mother and smiled. He made a decision.

"Che stai pensando Nicola?"

"I thought we could go and visit Nectarios at the cemetery tomorrow."

"Did many people come to his funeral?"

"Many. I'll take you after breakfast."

Nicola found a park close to Seventh Avenue. He pointed out the spot to his Mother. The granite headstone stood up and Nicola inspected it, happy with the result. His picture leapt out at Lidia and Nicola brought her a chair from the car to sit by his side. She tried to read the engraving but struggled. Nicola read it to her:

Lovingly remembered.
Husband to Lidia and Father to Nicola.
Nectarios Petrakis
2nd November 1951 - 31st October 2014

They sat until Lidia shivered as the shade came across. She got up and stood on the area to the left of Nectarios, stepping gently on the grass.

"Put me here when I go, Ok Nicola? Promise me."

"I promise, Mum."

71

Claudio wanted to leave, his prickly attitude irritating the nurses. His cardiologist arrived late, apologising with extravagant hand gestures. He looked at Claudio's observations, felt his pulse and smiled.

"Mr Claudio, you recovered much quicker than I expected. You can go home. Can someone look after you at home?"

"Yes, a friend."

The doctor winked. "Ok, I understand. A word of warning; no hanky-panky for at least four weeks."

"Hanky what?"

"You know, sex."

"Why didn't you just say sex?"

"To Claudio's further irritation, he held up four fingers. Four weeks from today. The hospital will make some rehabilitation appointments for you to make you stronger. I recommend you keep your appointments, so this doesn't happen again OK?"

Stronzo. "Of course, Doctor."

"Ok, the nurse and pharmacist will be here to give your medications and then discharge you. Good luck Mr Claudio."

He bristled and waited for the pharmacist. She arrived and went through the new profile of blood thinners, beta blockers and cholesterol tablets. Her cheeriness irritated Claudio, before a stern look made him realise what a crank he was.

"I'm sorry. I just want to go home." He smiled, hoping his apology was sufficient.

She smiled back and tapped his forearm. "We all do, Claudio. Now, in case you are taking Viagra, I recommended you stop it for at least three months or until your cardiologist says it is safe."

Lo sapevo, minchia. I fucking knew it. One says four weeks, this one three months. Another stern look came and he looked away.

He collected his medications and waited for Nicola to drive him home, where Gabriella served lasagne for them. He ate two mouthfuls and excused himself to bed. He slept for twelve hours and woke weak but refreshed.

Gabriella took him to his first rehab session a week later. He actually enjoyed hydrotherapy and the counselling. By the third week, Gabriella let him drive himself. His strength began to return. Gabriella started cooking more healthy meals for him. Their relationship, now platonic, was based on a sense of duty and mutual respect. She thought that if only he were twenty years younger, hell, even fifteen, this could work.

Claudio expressed his thanks daily to her and brought her flowers. His body had changed and despite being six kilos lighter, his muscular strength surprised his rehab physio. He was ready.

72

After a long day catching up on a backlog of rescheduled clients, Nicola needed rest. His phone beeped and it was Zivkovic.

"How's the counselling going?"

"Ten on the trot today. Getting my hours in."

"Don't let the hipsters burn you out. Look, I need your help with a man up on rape charges, seventeen in fact. High up in academia. He has pleaded guilty, but the Director of Public Prosecutions wants a psychological evaluation on him to help with sentencing. Five-day turnaround. Are you up for it? I'll be sitting in with you."

Nicola took a deep breath. "Sure, when?"

"Can you be at St Kilda Road tomorrow afternoon at three? That should give you enough time to read through the case. I'll renew your access and email you everything."

"Ok, thanks."

"Buzz me and I'll let you in."

He arrived early and sat thinking how he would do this. He had more facial hair than he did that day, his hair longer. His clothes were darker too. Zivkovic met him in the foyer and walked him through the process. He looked at Kondos through the one-way window of the interview room. His eyes were sunken and his stubble greyer than the man in lycra months ago. Zivkovic reminded Nicola that although no verdict hung on his report, that he should approach this as any other assessment. He introduced him from the other side of the table. An officer stood behind Kondos. Zivkovic introduced himself and Nicola.

"Mr Kondos, although you have pleaded guilty, the Director of Public Prosecutions has requested a psychological report." said Zivkovic.

As Zivkovic spoke, Nicola met Kondos' eyes and relaxed his facial features to show passivity. He read Kondos' face. He couldn't be sure that Kondos didn't recognise him, before remembering with relief that their eyes never met that day. He replayed the phone conversation with Kondos in his head and remembered he spoke, far quicker than his normal speech pattern. Nevertheless, he told himself to speak slowly.

"Dr Kondos, tell us about these interactions with your students." began Nicola.

"Where did you study?" asked Kondos.

"Masters of Psychology, University of Melbourne."

"I wanted to be sure you were qualified and not some hack."

"Ok, now we've established that, tell us about the interactions-"

"It won't make a difference, all this. It may be a procedural requirement, but will it help lower my sentence?" He placed his hands on his face like Shirley Temple, shook his head and spoke in a dull metallic voice.

"I'm remorseful, I did wrong the wrong thing and I've ruined my career. There, write that and be done with it. This is all psychobabble anyway."

"You used to say anatomy is integral to psychology, Dr Kondos."

"So I did teach you at some point. I thought I recognised you."

Zivkovic made eye contact with the officer behind Kondos and he shuffled a step closer.

"I married a great wife, had two lovely little girls, but somewhere along the way, I realised I shouldn't have gotten married. We ticked off the petty aspirations of our time; a great house in a great area, nice cars, good schools, minimal financial stress but I endured a boring, mind numbing family existence. Only my academic work mattered. Then, even that became stale. The first time a student came begging for special consideration, I felt powerful. They saw me as a God."

"Cheree Rivers came to you first. What happened?" asked Nicola.

"She did very well in dissection but bombed her first-semester exam. Anxiety got the better of her. She needed over eighty percent to pass that final year and she thought she wouldn't pass. I offered her a way out. The law calls it rape but like all the others, a simple quid pro quo."

Arrogant bastard, using my line, thought Nicola. He gave Kondos a vanilla face.

Zivkovic leaned forward. "What do all rapes have in common?"

"What?" replied Kondos, smirking.

"All rape is about power, Dr Kondos. Did you not use your power for sexual gratification?"

"I used my position to get what I wanted. Cheree got what *she* wanted; a pass."

"And how did that end for her?"

"She passed with flying colours," said Kondos with a smirk.

"She committed suicide three months later."

Kondos looked at both men and smirked some more. "And I'm supposed to feel what, responsible? There were clearly other stresses in her life. She was a neurotic."

"Was she a neurotic when she came to you? Did you sense her anxiety?"

"Yes, it was clear."

"And yet knowing this, you leveraged the situation, raped her and recorded it for posterity. Does that not extend this beyond a quid pro quo to premeditated perversion, Dr Kondos?" asked Nicola.

"I recall each one. Whether I recorded it or not is immaterial. They are all stored up here." he said, pointing to his temple.

"Tell me about your childhood. Was it a happy home?"

"In bits and pieces. I learned the art of being in my own world very early. But again - is this going to help beyond making you feel like you've ticked a box?"

Nicola persisted.

"Were you closer to your Mum or Dad?"

"I've said all I'm going to say, gentlemen."

Nicola wanted to piece together a thumbnail sketch of Kondos' childhood, even for his own curiosity, but was inclined to agree with him. He tried to fill the gaps from police interviews of his remaining family. His brother Gerry came across as resentful yet apathetic about his brother, noting only that, "he got the best of everything and he still squandered it." His Mother, an outwardly religious woman, remained aghast that her son could have done these things. He grew up in a loving Christian home, she said, conveniently omitting the frequent drunken bouts of her husband, the many times he beat her without opposition or resistance from either son. The interview with Stagan proved the most revealing, his recounting of Kondos' anger and petulance at not being handed back his position of head of anatomy sticking out in his mind. Other staff members recalled scenarios where he displayed contempt beyond arrogance towards students and colleagues alike.

Nicola looked at Zivkovic and nodded. "I think we're done here." The men got up to leave.

"He's quite the psychopath." said Zivkovic after they shut the door.

"Many boys grew with their brains saturated by serotonin, many never heard the word no, and many witness violence in their home. But they don't all rape women and justify it afterwards. He's cut up because he got caught. To him, someone broke a secret pact."

Nicola wrote the report that night and finally collapsed in a heap after three a.m. His sessions started at midday and he craved sleep without crows or other archetypes.

73

Claudio sat next to Lidia and waited until she woke from her post-breakfast nap. Her naps were more frequent, and she was eating more. She woke and peered at Claudio.

"Perche' sei tagliato a metà?"
Why are you cut in half?

She looked around the room and looked puzzled. Half the room disappeared. An MRI and some basic neurological testing showed the cancer marching through her left optic radiations, causing her to lose the right side of her vision. They moved her bed to the right wall, so the room was to her left, which made her more at ease and less paranoid about her surroundings. Nicola wondered how long before other functions deserted her.

Gabriella had been off work for about a month as she avoided Ivan and helped Claudio after his heart attack. Claudio would be home soon, and she wanted to get out before she went mad.

Ivan waited from ten till midday for Gabriella to arrive at the brothel, before losing patience and screeching out. Claudio followed him, watching as he met with three men at a cafe in North Fitzroy before returning home.

Claudio assessed the house as Ivan went in; single front brick with a small path down the side. Rear entry via a cobbled laneway led to a small concrete area and a large garage that fit three cars with ease. He returned home and told Gabriella to pack for two days. He surprised her with a weekend away to Venus Bay, with a beautiful two-bedroom apartment that looked back towards Inverloch and the Bass Strait. She sat in the spa and relaxed while Claudio caught fish off the beach a few hundred metres away. He returned and admired her on a chaise lounge sipping white wine.

"What a picture; you, relaxed."

"You're too good to me."

"I would say the same about you. This is the least I could do to say thank you."

"I can't stay with you forever Claudio. You're feeling better. Ivan must have moved on."

"I know; let's say another week or two. Is that too much to ask of you? I understand if you want to go back to your apartment."

She enjoyed the warm breeze and sipped the wine. "No, you're not being unreasonable." She got up and took Claudio by the hand and danced to a song in her head. She lowered her hand between his legs and smiled.

"No Viagra, no worries." she whispered into his ear. She led him inside and pushed him onto the bed.

"Should I check with my cardiologist?" asked Claudio

Gabriella took off her clothes and pointed at him, smiling. "Relax, I know CPR: Claudio. Please. Relax."

Later, he cooked her prawns and octopus the way he enjoyed them in Taormina. Extra virgin olive oil, parsley, garlic, lemon juice, salt and pepper.

They walked the beach the next morning, relaxed in the spa and drove back that night. The next morning, Gabriella woke late. Claudio was gone.

Ivan was a man of routine. He met the same men, talked the same shit and smoked the same number of cigarettes as the first time. Claudio repeated the routine for the next five days. He alternated between observing from inside and outside the car. Every second day he collected an envelope. After each period of surveillance, he visited Lidia.

A week passed since their time away. It was only two days, but it energised Claudio and gave calm to Gabriella. They sat over pasta, and to an observer they could have been Father and daughter.

"Gabriella, I want you to stay here as long as you need to, but you need to go back to your own place. This...situation, it is not real."

To Gabriella, this day was inevitable. She needed to return to real life, but part of her resented it. "I'll get my stuff ready. Is tomorrow Ok?"

"Whenever you are ready. Look, this is difficult for me too. I have enjoyed our time together."

"Well, we've said it now. One of us was going to say it, so it doesn't matter who. The quicker the better or we'll get awkward. Help me move back in tomorrow, will you?"

"Of course." Claudio stared at the floor.

"I'm sorry Claudio, I didn't mean it like that. I don't want to drag it out."

"Relax, I understand."

She packed her things in the hallway by ten the next morning and by midday, she was back at her flat. They went out to lunch and rested.

"Why don't you go and visit Lidia this afternoon?"

"Good idea. I'll see you later on then?"

He went to kiss her, but she turned her cheek and they backed away before leaning back in.

"I'm sorry. Let's do this properly, Claudio."

Gabriella kissed him on the lips and lingered in his protective embrace before backing away.

"I'll call you soon I promise." said Claudio.

"Please do. I still want to see you sometimes. Stay healthy."

Claudio caressed the back of her head and took in her face. He stored the image and held onto it.

He drove to the nursing home and placed his phone in a groove under the oak bench seat that was concealed. He returned home and collected his pre-prepared bag. Driving past the cobbled laneway at the back of Ivan's house, he found a parking spot he was happy with, draped by low branches of the tree nearest to it. The gate lock was easy to free up and the garage door lifted with little pressure. He rested Ivan's tracking device on top of the fridge and switched it on. He itched in the overalls but left them on and looked around the garage. He looked at his watch, four-thirty, and rested his loaded carbine shotgun on the bench. He buried it in his garage for years under thick plastic and no dust had any chance of getting into it. It was as smooth and new as the last time he used it to hunt twenty years ago with Nectarios and he maintained it well. In the third drawer, he found three handguns. He was more comfortable with his carbine. He wasn't prone to whimsy or being side-tracked but liked the idea of using Ivan's own gun on him as the perfect idea of justice. He tested each, selected the smoothest firing one, found a clip for it and loaded it.

> *Claudio sat two tables away from Lidia and her three female friends. Her parents allowed her to go out when she turned eighteen, as long as Claudio chaperoned them. As they finished their coffee, three men joined their table and struck up a conversation. The tallest one got too close for Lidia's liking and she pushed him away, which only encouraged him more. Claudio stayed put but made the slightest eye contact with her, a sign for the girls to get up to leave. They bid the men goodnight. The tallest one shook hands with Lidia and turned to his friends. "Questa la spacco in due". I'd break her in half. The group joined in raucous laughter and ordered drinks. Claudio got up without making it clear he was with them. He drove the girls home and returned to park behind the row of cafes. They were still there, and he waited as they drank rounds of Amaro Averna.*

Entitled brats from rich parents, he thought to himself. As they went their separate ways, he followed the tall one. The man's gait deteriorated as he cut through the park before Claudio caught up with him.

"You like my sister?"

"Sorry?" he said, facing him. He was calm from the Averna but Claudio's face unsettled him.

"Do you like her or not?"

"Sure, but-"

"But what? You got so close to her, it seemed that you liked her. Come to my house and meet her. Come?" Claudio smiled.

"Ok."

"What's your name?"

"Vito. Vito Semola." He began to sweat, and his head started to spin a little. He tried to calculate how distant the lights of the cafes and bars were from their brightness. He strained to hear the chatter, the cars and got silence in return.

The next sound was the strike of Claudio's wooden truncheon against the skull on the back of the head. His eyes rolled for a second before

*the lights went out. Claudio carried him with ease
to his car and drove to the clifftops overlooking
the Strait of Messina. A car was leaving, and he
took the opportunity to drive onto a narrow,
grassed area alongside a row of bushes. He took
his shoes off and lifted the still comatose Vito
from the car, took his jacket off and lay it and the
grass away from the edge. He stood Vito up and
slapped him awake. As Vito's eyes opened,
Claudio walked him across to the edge, his
footprints easy to see in the dirt, before pushing
him onto the rocks and foaming waves below. His
body made a dull thud, coming to rest a metre
from the water, waves now crashing onto him.*

*The news of his death shocked the island, but
police were quick to attribute the death to alcohol
after an autopsy and discovering footprints at the
lookout above. Public service announcements
about the dangers of alcohol were spread
throughout the island. Witnesses had seen him
drinking round after round with friends before
stumbling towards the park.*

*Some weeks later, Claudio and Lidia boarded a
ship for Australia. An uncle had agreed to
sponsor them and sent money for their fares.
Many men besotted by Lidia's blue eyes and
blonde hair dared not venture beyond wild
thoughts as Claudio hawked her every move.*

Ivan saw the alert on his phone. His smiled as his house showed up on the GPS. *Come back, have you bitch?* He drove the five minutes home, got out and walked quickly up and down the street to find Gabriella's car. He then ran down the side street and found nothing. His phone rang and he ripped it out.

"Ivan, Besut here. I've got your money." said a breathless voice.

"About fucking time, you monkey. Be here in an hour."

He walked back towards the back gate and smiled when he saw it ajar. Claudio heard the gate creak, clicked the safety off the carbine and slowed his breathing like he did when he hunted. Ivan lifted the garage door with a clang and walked into the centre of the floor.

"Come out Gabriella, I know you're in here."

The tracker beeped again. He turned towards the fridge, picked up the tracker and threw it at the wall, smashing it to pieces.

"No way out, bitch, you hear me?"

He pulled down the garage door with force. As the door's loud clang echoed, the first shell shattered his left ankle. He hopped on his right and collapsed, hit the concrete floor hard, his anguished cry reverberating. Claudio stepped out and shot the other ankle and knocked Ivan out with the butt of the gun to the head as he wailed in pain. He tied his hands together, hitched the knot tight to the bull bar of the 4WD and stuffed a rag in his mouth. From the freezer, he grabbed the two bags with ice he brought, made cuts down the centres and rested an ankle on each, before splashing his face with a bucket of cold water. Ivan woke and blacked out from the immediate rush of pain. He came in and out of consciousness before waking to even more pain. Shhh said Claudio, his finger over his lips.

"Don't force yourself. It will only hurt more." He walked around the room, Ivan's eyes following him. Claudio returned, knelt before him and spoke in a soft voice.

"Gabriella; a gem of a woman like this you have and how do you treat her? You hit her, bruise her, a woman? You are no man. Promise me she will be safe from you." said Claudio.

"I...I promise." spluttered Ivan, blood mixed with saliva,, his breathing too fast to talk as his body began to shake, his eyes now barely able to stay open from the blood loss.

He walked over to Ivan's gun and took off the safety. "Look at me." he said. He pressed the gun hard into the skin, midway between his eyes, kept it there for an eternity, leaving a perfect indentation. He backed it away and Ivan looked at him, relief showing on his face before Claudio fired at the indentation, leaving a starfish pattern in his now slumped head. He walked out of the garage, left the gloves on, took off the overalls, changed shoes

and bagged them. He drove around, found Ivan's car
with the remote and placed his keys and gun inside the
glovebox. He drove to a car wash near his home with no
CCTV and dumped overalls, gloves and shoes in
different bins. He drove back to the home and collected
his phone before walking in to see Lidia. He stayed half
an hour until she fell asleep.

Later, he knelt on his bed before Morena's portrait and
kissed the left part of her neck. His pulse rose to 135 in
the garage and his body ached from exertion. He took a
long bath and found no trouble sleeping.

A tardy Besut Azargam knocked on Ivan's door, an
envelope laden with twelve grand sitting fat in his left
hand. *Two thousand interest on ten you Jahash bastard*
he said to himself. He waited five minutes and left a text
and message on his voicemail.

It took two days for someone to find Ivan's body. His
sister checked in on him after countless phone calls to let
him know their Father had died from a stroke. She found
his body after seeing the gate ajar. She was surprised by
the sense of relief that hit her before any shock could
take over. No grief came, not even with the violent image
confronting her to force any emotional rebalancing of the
ledger. He estranged himself from the family, and after
many attempts to reconcile they gave up. Threatening to
kill his parents was the last straw and backspaced over
any warm childhood memories. He was a hand grenade
with the safety pin pulled; it was only a matter of when
he would explode, not if.

Zivkovic arrived half an hour after the forensic team began to work. They used Ivan's fingerprint on his phone. Within an hour they located the hapless Besut, whose stuttering and jitteriness made him a suspect to be eliminated. The fat wallet and a stolen handgun under his car seat didn't help matters.

"Twelve grand in this envelope. Did you owe Ivan money?" asked the officer.

"Yyy-ee-sss," he said, shaking. "He leant me ten two weeks ago."

"Two grand interest on ten; not very friendly rates, are they?"

"I never said he was my friend."

"I'm curious how you made up the interest, but we'll get to that later." He stepped away as a trail of piss trickled from Besut towards him.

Zivkovic rang them to bring Besut around the back to the garage. When he shook and shrieked upon seeing the body, he knew he wasn't involved. His phone's GPS showed him at Ivan's address for five minutes, forty-five seconds. Hardly enough time to stun Ivan, tie him up, execute him and place Ivan's own gun and keys in his car. A long barrel gun was used on the ankles and a handgun for the head shot. Zivkovic thought that someone Besut's age wouldn't know what a long-barrelled gun looked like or how to operate it. Besut didn't seem capable of planning anything more than a trip to the supermarket.

Zivkovic rang Nicola and asked him to join them. "I've got a situation here. I could use your eyes."

Nicola looked at the scene and worked backwards; the body's final position, initial blood spill pattern and direction, rough footprints in the bathroom, gate latch broken. He crouched down near the footprints, careful not to disturb them and imagined the angle Claudio had.

"Well?"

"Well, he waited here, took the first shot, hit his left ankle?"

"Are you asking me or telling me?"

"There are bits of bone scattered in the blood spill closest to the bathroom. The left ankle was a perfect shot, plenty of time to aim. He then walked out and got a more hurried shot on the right and immobilise him before he made too much noise. The shot was more tangential and while there is more blood, not as much bone. Then he hits him with the butt of the gun, knocks him out and secures him to the bullbar. He props up the ankles on the ice packs on to stop him bleeding out too fast. He wants him alive for the final shot and eye contact before he teased him with a press. And then bang."

Zivkovic looked at him and frowned. The pair of forensic officers nodded in agreement to Zivkovic. Nicola looked through the drawers along the side of the garage. He found a box with over a hundred thousand dollars, the gun drawer and looked up. "This was no gang or revenge kill Stefan, this was personal. Money's untouched. Nicola walked around the garage and retraced his steps. "What kind of criminal wanting to take out a rival uses a long barrel to shoot his ankles, uses the victim's own handgun to shoot him in the head and leaves money behind?" Before Zivkovic could answer, Nicola looked back at Ivan's forehead, looked at the faint smudge running sideways and came back at him. "He wiped blood from the entry wound to make it look clean and symmetrical."

"And?"

"Almost whimsical, like an artist touching up a painting."

Nicola called the clinic and asked them to drop his bookings from three days to two. Zivkovic handed him some notes and asked him to talk to the girlfriend. The name stood out: Gabriella Mancuso. Nicola asked what nationality Ivan was.

"Constantin. Sounds Romanian if I'm not mistaken."

75

Nicola spent the evening by his Mother's side. He brought in some arancini left in the fridge and Lidia enjoyed them. As he settled her back into bed, she turned to him. Her eyes looked duller and her cheekbones were more prominent.

"*Sto morendo*, Nicola."
I'm dying.

Her voice was more of a wheeze now, her control of her larynx diminishing.

"Mum no, come on-"

"Shh. Your Mother is talking. Before I am *muta*, let me talk. My brain is like a house. Someone is going *click* one room after another room is dark. I feel pain, but no fear, *nessuna paura* Nicola. When enough rooms are dark, I want to go. Promise me. Please, let me go."

Her eyes, her upturned palms implored him. She looked at the ceiling as if Nicola was no longer present.

She did not recall that Nicola was her medical power of attorney. When Nectarios' condition rendered Nectarios a shell of the man Lidia knew, she asked Nicola to be her power of attorney. Iain Grafton drew up the documents.

As they signed, she turned to Nicola.

"Se non riesco a respirare, rispondere o mangiare senza macchine, non voglio vivere, mi devi spegnere."

"Mum says if she can't breathe, respond or eat on her own, she wants to be switched off."

"A DNR?" Grafton asked.

"Yes."

Grafton went through the list of scenarios: breathe without a ventilator, eat without assistance, be in unbearable pain that is unmanageable with medication-"

Lidia, exasperated, stopped him. "Iain, Nicola will know when, OK?"

Nicola nodded, and Iain added the DNR clause after they agreed on the wording.

He never told Claudio. Now it was time. He drove to Claudio's house and Claudio answered in a long sleeve flannel shirt marked with old paint.

"Didn't you visit Lidia tonight?"

"I went before, then I got busy with this." he said, pointing to the hallway. Claudio had thrown himself into repainting the house. Most of his belongings were either in boxes or stacked into the middle of rooms.

"Now you decide to paint the house?"

"Yes Nicola, now. While I'm still young."

"We need to talk about Lidia. She is talking about the end of her life and there's something you need to know."

"Ok, go on."

"She asked me three years ago when Dad was going through his chemo to be her power of attorney."

"I know this." he said, irritated.

"Hang on. She also wanted to refuse treatment where it might leave her unable to look after her own function, breathing, eating, respond, that we refuse treatment."

"*Che cazzo*, what do you mean refuse treatment? We put her to sleep like a dog?"

"Not so long ago you wanted me to be your power of attorney and switch you off if you were where Lidia was, remember?"

"I was emotional, Nicola. You cannot be serious that we switch her off."

"Mum wanted me to do this when she was of sound mind. This was way before her dementia hit her. She won't remember it now, but she asked me to do this. It is only if something urgent happens that I would decide. She is dying Zio, and she knows it. She talks about lights in her brain switching off one by one. She knows this much,"

Claudio edged closer to him and raised his finger.

"You are a great son to your Mother and Father Nicola, so what I am going to say to you, I say with love. You will not do anything like what you are saying while I am able to stop it. You may be her power of attorney, but I am her brother. I stopped anything bad happening to her in Sicily, on the boat and to the day I walked her into the church to marry your Father. You would not be here without me protecting her, remember that. The paper means nothing to me. Now let me finish sugar soaping the walls before I get too tired."

Nicola knew better than to reason further and left.

76

Gabriella answered her phone and didn't recognise the number.

"Nicola here, Gabriella."

"Hi - everything OK?"

"I work with Victoria Police, so this is an official call. Ivan's dead."

"How?"

"Tied up and shot in his garage." A pause.

"How fitting."

"We need to talk. Can I meet you near your place?"

An hour later, they sat in a quiet booth in a cafe.

"Tell me about your movements three days ago."

"Claudio helped me move back into my flat. We had lunch and we rested there until three-thirty and then he left to see Lidia. After that, I went back to work. For a night shift."

"Ivan, did he have any enemies?"

"He sold drugs, leant money with high interest and on-sold stolen cars. He rubbed people up the wrong way. He got violent when people were late. Any number of people would want him dead."

"How did he tolerate you doing sex work?"

"I tolerated his way of life; he turned a blind eye to mine." Nicola's eyes narrowed. "Look, I know you're wondering what I was doing with him. I couldn't be the good Catholic virgin my parents wanted, so I left home. Ivan was the first man who treated me well, at first anyway. I should have left long ago"

"What made you finally leave him?"

She described the assault and he could see her fear. She pulled her top to the left, revealing the full extent of the still mottled area around her neck, the skin scarred at the margins. He concluded that she could not have done this. Attacking him in the heat of the moment maybe, but not a planned ambush and execution.

"There were other times we hit each other but they were mainly playful during sex. This was different."

"I'm sorry, Gabriella."

"Don't be," she said. "We carry these scars and move on. The story of time."

He drove and regretted neglecting his clients. A couple
made alternative arrangements after two rescheduled
appointments. He spent the first two minutes apologising
to each client. To his relief, most thought nothing of it.
Sario Florinos was back and booked his last slot.
Nicola's head was full and needed a rest.

"Long day Nicola?"

"My list got a little out of hand so I'm making up for it."

"What's been bugging you?"

Nicola smiled. "Hang on, you're paying to let me ask
you that question."

"And sometimes these are just chats between two men.
The therapeutic benefit doesn't show itself till later.
Come on, you can tell Uncle Sario."

He described the murder scene in Ivan's garage.

"So, to summarise: this man is shot in both ankles with a
long barrel shotgun, tied up, kept awake to draw out his
pain, then shot through the head exactly between the eyes
with a handgun. The blood is then wiped away from the
head wound?"

Nicola nodded.

"Ever heard of the Mark of Cain Nicola?"

"Yes. A symbol from God that protected-"

"Allow me, Nicola. *Genesis 4:15*: when Cain murdered Abel, he was forced to live a life as a wanderer, a nomad for life. But no one could harm him because they could see the mark given by God. His penance was the life without a family and land to base himself, and that he spent his time in shame and to repent."

"And the symmetry of the head wound?"

Florinos put his hand up. "Modern culture added that layer. Agatha Christie used it twice; in *Curtain*, where Poirot murdered serial killer Stephen Norton with a gunshot between the eyes before he himself died. Then Justice Wargrave in *And Then There Were None*, you know, the one where ten people invited to an island get bumped off one by one for their sins?"

"Yes, I remember that movie!" said Nicola, his eyes widening.

"Pfft - forget the movie, they bastardised the plot. The book, as always, is superior. The Judge killed everyone on the island and then faked his death with a revolver to make him look like one of the victims. As the last person on the island, he set up an elastic mechanism to leave the wound between the eyes. He wanted the case to be impossible to solve but couldn't help himself and left a note in a bottle. Both were symmetrical wounds inflicted by men whose morality made them think that they were somehow above the law. They exercised justice they knew normal society and laws could not deliver. Both left behind letters explaining why they did what they did and neither demanded sympathy."

He looked at Nicola and screwed his face up in a scowl. "Where did I lose you Nicola?"

"You make more sense than you realise."

"Oh, Ok, excellent." He beamed, very much happy with himself.

"As reward, a game of chess?"

"When things settle, I promise we will."

"You can start as white. I need practice playing as black."

77

Kondos was being briefed by the counsel provided by Legal Aid, a young and efficient man who tried to embrace this experience to use towards his aspirations of becoming a criminal lawyer. Victim impact statements and final sentencing were scheduled for the next day. Kondos stared into space as the young man summarised the process. He soon tuned out.

"Any questions, Dr Kondos?"

"None."

Kondos saw no point in fighting any more. He was furious at Olivia for turning him in after her promise but was not surprised when she did. The moment she dangled the USB in front of him, a sense of inevitability haunted him, not for the guilt, but being caught. He enjoyed and savoured every transaction with the girls that submitted to his power, authority and standing. No one could take those memories away, but it was time to pay.

Yvette Branders began her Victim Impact Statement by thanking the court for the opportunity to make their statement and welcoming the official apology from the faculty. She then turned to Kondos.

"What you did to me was to use your power to shrink and degrade me. I was vulnerable and you used that to your sick, perverted advantage. When you finished raping me, you told me that this was our secret, or else I would repeat the year. I can only speak for myself, but I have moved on from this, and the knowledge that you will be stripped of your privileges goes some way to giving me peace."

Faruz Nairi and Tran Phung were next. Both echoed Rivers' sentiments, but both women showed their intimidation by Kondos' presence and found it hard to make eye contact with him. Phung began crying as Kondos smiled to her.

Petra was next. She had no trouble making eye contact with him. She made sure to trace the area on her right temporal bone broken when Kondos hit the car on impact. Kondos felt a sharp pain in the area and bore down on it.

"Petra Rouveliotis."

Petra walked to the microphone and kept eye contact with him the whole way.

"Thank you, Your Honour. I reiterate my gratitude, both to the court for this opportunity. I also thank the faculty of medicine for their prompt acknowledgement and apology. An apology for something that, while taking place within their walls and jurisdiction, was not foreseeable. But such was the perversion of an individual that this was able to take place. I will never forget what happened that day, but I am stronger in spite of it. Mr

Kondos, for I will no longer address you by the title I addressed you with that day, I want you to look at me. Look. At. Me."

He tried to match her stare. He remembered her hospital visit, and after a second buckled and looked away, His right temple throbbed again and he rubbed it, grimacing.

"From our interaction that day, and by extension those with the other students whose rapes you have pleaded guilty to, it is logical in your mind that we were exchanging something. A simple transaction; sex for grades in your office where you used your power for your own perversion. In your mind, it was a fair trade. I came to you asking for advice and special consideration after the death of my uncle. He had suffered from cancer which affected my exam preparation. You made me wait and stew while you looked at my records, at length, drawing it out and amplifying my anxiety before proposing that we 'help each other'. I froze and you preyed on my mental paralysis and before I knew it you were inside me, like an animal. At what point did I offer consent for you to bend me over your desk, one hand pushing down my upper back while the other removed my jeans? Can you tell me and tell the court? I kicked away and escaped when I realised what was going on - when I sensed a moment where there was less pressure on my back. And I put the experience to the side long enough to study, study hard, study harder to forget and then pass. I passed well without your proposition, without your 'help'. I do not blame anyone who did not come forward. Like the others, I was trapped by the terrible experience you put us through. I do not want to disrespect the court and calling you a psychopath. But, in the absence of this conclusion, what other is there to make?"

"The trade-off for me was that you derailed my life. I went through depression and self-doubt, both of which will pay me visits again, I am sure. But you will atrophy. I and your other victims will deal with these memories but will prosper and enjoy our freedoms knowing that you are locked away, without freedoms, family, your livelihood, your academia, all gone."

She walked to the back of the court and sat with the other students. Last to present was Tessa Rivers, a tall, blonde woman who looked more in her mid-thirties. Judge Mary Castelan looked over her glasses and frowned as she looked at her written notes.

"Are you a victim as outlined in the charges against the defendant?" she asked.

"No, your honour. My name is Tessa Rivers. My sister was Cheree Rivers, the defendant's first victim as I understand it. I wanted to make a statement on behalf of my sister and our family."

Kondos stood.

"I object, Your Honour. This is bullshit!" yelled Kondos, catching his lawyer off guard. Judge Castelan ordered that he sit down and motioned for the two bailiffs to be closer at hand. Kondos sat and faced the wall opposite to the microphone.

"I'll allow it. Please continue." said Castelan.

Rivers sucked in two deep breaths.

"Cheree was tender and young, but at the same time, an old soul. As a thirteen-year-old she showed the maturity of someone far beyond her years. And yet she was as soft as a lamb. Her older brother and I were over fifteen years old when she was born, a little baby surprise that we cherished. She finished high school a month after her seventeenth birthday and put off celebrating her eighteenth birthday until she finished her first-year exams. In second year, she placed expectations on herself that were high, even for her. As a doctor myself, I remembered how difficult the course was, juggling disciplines that were difficult to grasp. For the first time, she was struggling. One day she visited me at my clinic. She was anxious and depressed. Where her studies made her thrive and push through her anxiety, now they were a crippling, heavy burden. She told me that she needed a final exam mark over eighty in anatomy to avoid repeating second year in full."

She stopped and let out an anguished cry.

"I told her to see her lecturer - you, in good time, for advice on how to approach the exams and act as a guide. Instead, you traded on her anxiety and raped her in your office, beneath your plaques, fellowships, your degrees

and your doctorate. The detective told us you raped her
and continued even after she said stop, even when she
was powerless to stop you. Cheree did not tell us
anything; she passed the year but far from relieved, she
felt more anxiety. A week later, we found her lifeless in
her bed. She took an overdose of Valium. The autopsy
said she died from respiratory failure, a slow death. What
you did was prey on a vulnerability in a student you had
a duty of care to help, to guide, not to rape. This has
affected us as a family in a way you will never
understand. There is no way to quantify the damage you
have caused. Our little lamb is gone. Every day I blame
myself for telling her to see you. Every day I live with it
and it hurts. No punishment will ever make that better. I
don't believe in rehabilitation for your kind. Although it
is an imperfect punishment in an imperfect world, you
having to live with yourself while other people heal is the
best we have. Society is better without you in it."

Tessa turned and sat with her brother. She buried her face
in his chest, spent. After a respectful period of silence,
Judge Castelan spoke with a soft voice.

"I wish to thank the brave women who have offered their
impact statements to the court. These are difficult
sentiments to deliver in any forum, and to do so is
something we never countenance. Sentencing will be a
week from today."

Nicola hugged his cousin. As Kondos was led away, he
stopped. Petra pulled away but it was too late. The dots
were joined in his head and he exploded with rage,

knocking one bailiff to the ground. He jerked away and ran at Nicola, but not fast enough as the other bailiff caught him, diving full stretch in mid-air and catching him around the waist. Kondos managed to get a handful of Nicola's shirt, before the other bailiff wrenched Kondos' other arm tight behind his back. The pair made short work of him, securing both hands behind his back and holding his head hard into the wooden floor.

"No trouble, Ok? Stop, let your body go limp and we'll all be fine. Promise?"

Kondos looked up at Nicola, veins straining through his skin, eyes bulging. "I should have killed you that day," he said before allowing his body to relax.

The bailiffs stood Kondos up, turned him away from Nicola and led him out of the courtroom. Nicola stood and watched them take him away, mute until Petra dragged him off the spot and outside where the cool air brought him back.

78

Lidia now spent more time sleeping than awake. When awake, her crippling headaches forced Dr Del Vecchio to move her onto mild opioids. As she slept, Nicola sat at the end of her bed with notes from the Ivan scene and his interview with Gabriella. The crime scene and the whole setup irritated him. No other leads proved helpful. Zivkovic was leaning towards putting it down to criminal revenge and devoting resources to that train of thought. Nicola remained dissatisfied, and his conversation with Sario Florinos kept cannoning through his head. Someone who considered themselves above the law, delivering justice.

Later that night, Lidia stirred and spoke in an agitated tone.

"Non gli far male Claudio, non mi toccava. No Claudio, no."
Don't hurt him, he meant no harm.

Lidia stirred, then woke, her eyes looking like she had seen a ghost.
"Nicola."

"Yes, Mum. Are you Ok?"

"Claudio gli ha fatto male."
Claudio hurt him.

"Who Mum? Who?"

"Solo mi parlava, non mi toccava. Ma lo gettò lo stesso sul mare."
He was only talking to me, not touching me. But he threw him overboard, into the sea all the same.

"I am hungry Nico," she said, coming back into the present.

Nicola arranged food and ate with his Mother. She ate slower now and stopped after only one or two mouthfuls. He focused on the quality time left. No one could say he hadn't been a good son his parents. Some level of guilt nagged at him for the distractions that stopped him seeing his Mother more now she was deteriorating. Claudio came less often and by himself.

A few days later, she began experiencing violent episodes of vomiting and refused to eat. The headaches became more intense and Lidia became more agitated.

Nicola knocked on Claudio's door and smelt strong paint fumes. He opened and was ready to go.

"I wanted us to talk before we met with Del Vecchio and Marco. Mum is in a lot of pain. We should bring her home. She should be at home."

Claudio looked at his nephew. "I can stay over too if you like. This bloody painting can wait"

"She's your sister. Please, stay. We may not have a lot of time with her."

They sat opposite Del Vecchio and Marco and explained their wishes. They made the palliative care arrangements. Lidia slept in her own bed for the first time that night in over a year. Nicola blocked out appointments while he coordinated Lidia's care. Alex rang, and told him that H, while concerned, was understanding. Nicola suggested she stay away as Claudio was staying.

Marco kindly arranged to let Pina stay and care for Lidia. Her speech was slurred and her breathing more laboured. On the third night, Lidia grabbed Pina's arm with a strength that made her catch her breath.

"Tell me, Lidia."

"*Domani figlia me ne vado.*"
Tomorrow child, I'm leaving.

She remembered the same words from her Nonna as a twelve-year-old. She remembered anecdotes of people who knew when they were going to leave the earth they walked upon. The proclamation sat somewhere between witchery and instinct, yet it was neither. Her Mother and aunts forbade her to sit with her Nonna as she died, but she snuck in and watched, transfixed. Consumed with her Nonna, no one paid attention to her. She sat with Lidia until she slept and broke the news to Nicola and Claudio.

"Zia Rosa told us the same thing when she died," said Claudio. "So, this is it."

Nicola slept on the floor under his Mother and lay listening to every breath. She slept next to him during the night terrors as a six-year-old and then again as an eight-year-old. He cried at the symmetry and cruelty of it all. The clock read 5.47 a.m. when she called Nectarios' name; her last word. Delirium was in full swing as neural pathways short-circuited, her brain's final phase. Nicola checked her pulse when he woke and pulled a chair to sit next to her. Claudio brought coffee in and sat next to him.

They sat with Lidia for the rest of the day. Pina came in after lunch and they sat around her, talking about her while her body made plans to leave. She stopped talking and was unresponsive, though her pulse remained stable at fifty. Her pain was being well managed. They resigned themselves to the fact that she was as comfortable as possible, that nothing more could be done and waited.

Nicola stepped out of the room, expecting the crows. A pair perched on duty above her window. Nicola traded stares with them before going back inside. He lay next to her, in the same spot where Nectarios exhaled for the last time. He held her hand and it felt cold. Her pulse dropped below thirty. A few minutes later, the heart rate monitor line flattened. They stayed with her, silent.

Crowded House's 'Catherine Wheels' played through Nicola's head:

She's gone
Vanished in the night
Broke off the logic of light

No immediate tears flowed, only suspended emotion as
each of them sat and reflected, each in their own way
staring death in the face before looking away. Tears
finally came, and Nicola realised he was alone; the two
people who brought him into the world now gone.

79

Gianpiero Biscano arrived an hour later. He sighed and embraced Nicola.

"Nicola, my deepest sympathies. After your Father, I didn't expect to see you again so soon."

"Thank you Signor Biscano, me neither."

"Brutta vita."

He drove with Claudio to the home in the morning to discuss the arrangements. They drove back along Bell St as the sun darted in and out of the clouds.

"How is Gabriella?" asked Nicola.

"I have not spoken to her since she went back to her apartment. We needed some time apart after everything."

"Has Ivan tried to contact her?"

"I hope not."

"He hasn't." Nicola pulled over.

"How do you know?" asked Claudio, his body betraying him as his head cocked at a slight angle and his shoulders tensed up.

"Ivan's dead, Claudio. Shot through the head. Ankles too. But the head wound was interesting. Whoever killed him used a long barrel, an old-style carbine they reckon, to shoot his ankles, then tied him up and used his own gun to shoot him exactly between the eyes. He wiped the blood away from the entrance would to make it look clean." Nicola pointed his index finger hard into the spot and saw Claudio's expression. *Bingo.*

"What do they call that, the mark in the centre of the forehead?"

"*Boh*, what?"

"The Mark of Cain. *Il Marchio di Caino*; a strong symbol so symmetrical, so exact, by someone who thought only they could give justice."

Claudio bowed his head in resignation before meeting his eyes. "He hit her, Nicola. He was brutal. He would have hurt her again. At my age, we could not be together. If I was younger...but I did not trust him to leave her alone. I am not going to be around to protect her forever."

"Was it because she looked like Morena?"

He waved the comparison away. "Come on, I thought you were smarter than that, Nicola. God gave Morena no chance. I could not just let Gabriella's life destroyed by that *figlio di mignotta.*"

Nicola thought that he killed Ivan out of jealousy and that Gabriella was a proxy for Morena. He was wrong.

"I understand."

"I must pay. Whether I say goodbye to my sister at the funeral home or at the funeral, it's in your hands, Nicola. But I ask you to let me bury her, please."

He thought hard and his head hurt. Hurrying the process for a funeral two days away to allow Claudio to say goodbye proved a great inconvenience for Signor Biscano, but he had tolerated worse. Rationalising the issue was difficult, but he owed it to his uncle. He placed no funeral notice and only called those close to her. Claudio and Nicola were her only family in Australia.

80

Kondos slumped into his seat at the front of the court. He got up again as Judge Castelan walked to her chair.
Nicola sat on the opposite side from Petra, Tessa, Faruz, Tran and Yvette, who sat together as the Judge spoke.

"Mr Kondos, please stand."

She continued. "Raised in a strict yet loving family environment, you showed early signs of academic excellence. With hard work and immense dedication, you obtained a position of respect and authority within one of Australia's elite medical teaching schools. You had a well-structured home life to balance your demanding academic one; a loving wife and two beautiful girls, and no overbearing financial issues. It is both difficult and distressing to believe that against this background and with no past criminal history that these heinous acts happened."

She paused. Kondos' face was blank.

"In your position of Head of Anatomy, you were aware of your role in upholding and maintaining a duty of care for students. Since time immemorial, students, even you, have experienced stress and a sense of struggle at some stage. But rather than offer sympathy and educational assistance, or some consideration of their circumstances, you cornered them into sexual acts. Not content with this, you recorded and documented these rapes on USB storage devices. This makes the act more depraved, the need to document your perversion. You viewed these planned transactions as equal and fair. But rape is about power; in this case both academic and physical. Your predetermination to commit these acts indicates an absence of remorse. It leads me to question your place in society without thoughts of committing such acts again entering your head, given the chance. You have foregone your place in society, let alone as someone with authority in a teaching institution. The victim impact statements confirm this to me and underline your callousness and serial opportunism. I am relieved for your wife and daughters that you are out of their lives. I hope that they can move on from this."

She paused again, this time in deference to the victims.

"I am not inclined to harbour any thoughts of you acquiring respect for anyone else but yourself., and accordingly, I am sentencing you to 27 years, with no eligibility for parole during this time."

After the previous incident, the bailiffs positioned themselves much closer to Kondos and took no chances. No expressions of delight or whooping came from the observers, just relief. The five students hugged, left the court and returned to their lives.

81

Nicola knocked on the door to wake his uncle. Nicola had insisted he stay until the funeral. After three knocks and no response, his mind raced to the worst. At last, the door opened. His uncle was shaven and wearing his undershirt, his dark blue shirt open, unbuttoned.

"Zio,-"

"Nicola, please. I had no idea ten years, what am I saying, ten weeks ago that we would be burying my sister, your Mother and handing myself in for murder. But today is about your Mother, my sister She deserves respect today. So, let's give her that respect. After, we do what we need to do."

They drank coffee and ate toast before leaving. At the church, Petra and Sia sat in the front row. Nicola chose not to tell Rita anything. Three rows back, Marco, Pina and Dr Del Vecchio waved to him. Nicola coaxed them to the front. At the back, tucked away in the corner sat Gina, in a black jacket and pants, her hair bundled tight. Nicola turned and looked at her for an eternity, before waving her closer. She sat two rows behind, unsure, before Nicola moved across for her and waved her to come and sit.

"Are you sure?" she whispered, still hesitant. She tried to hush the racing of her heart in spite of the occasion.

"Please."

The priest conducted a short service. Del Vecchio, Pina, Marco, Claudio and Nicola walked Lidia to the hearse. Today was bright, with high and wispy cirrus clouds. A light breeze blew. Lidia loved days like this.

They drove the short distance to MacPherson St. Lidia was lowered, reunited at last with Nectarios. Gina's hand wrapped itself around his, her grip tentative, almost infant like in pressure. Her grip became firmer as his hand enclosed hers. A warm feeling passed through their hands and he squeezed a little tighter. Gina began to cry. He brought her in close and kissed her head, his tears now dripping onto her black hair, falling like rain into soil.

They ate lunch at The Kent on Rathdowne St. The table at the back was quiet between the grief of Lidia and the uncertainty between him and Gina. After some food, they chatted over coffee about Lidia and Nectarios, most of the memories coming from the era before their collective illnesses. *That feels like centuries ago* thought Nicola. Gina squeezed his hand under the table and mouthed *are you OK?* He nodded. Claudio stood and started talking. His words cut through the conversation. Everybody stopped and turned to him.

"Your parents were beautiful people. I am biased of course, but they worked hard for those people they loved. Nectarios raised you, Sia, and your sister. They put up with me after Morena died. And they raised you, Nicola.

Through good and bad, they stayed together and made more than what they could do apart. You understand, Nicola?"

Nicola blushed. Gina looked at her watch and said goodbye to everyone. She was near the door when she looked back, waved and kept walking out onto the street. A uniform chorus of disdain came as Nicola stayed rooted to the spot.

"Get up, *stronzo*." said Claudio, pointing with urgency to the door.

Nicola looked at Sia.

"Don't look into my eyes, look into hers. Go." said Sia. Petra jerked her head in Gina's direction.

He caught up to her and grabbed her arm.

"Yes?"

"I'm sorry Gina."

She backhanded Nicola across the chest.

"Firstly, call me Gigi. That's what you used to call me. *Gi-Gi*. When you called me Gina that day it was like you were talking to another woman. It drove me mad and you knew it. Say it."

"Gigi, I'm sorry. I was cruel to you."

She dragged him by the hand across the road to Curtain Park where they sat on a bench, blown by the gentle breeze.

"I know, and I deserved it. What did Claudio say? Do you think Nectarios and Lidia never fought, never wanted to kill each other? They fought because they didn't want to fight with anyone else. No one else would have them, Nicola. I don't want to fight with anyone else. I have some explaining to do and I will do that. But only if you promise to fight with me forever until we are also underground - together. I need that from you, Nicola. No one goes through life undamaged. How many wogs our age get to go through this with another person who understands? I don't want to atrophy alone and neither do you. Do you?"

"Well, no. Not if you're offering-"

"Right then. Does Lidia's *Gaggia* still work?"

"Of course."

"I will see you tomorrow after breakfast for coffee. By after breakfast, I mean ten."

Nicola's heart almost burst through his chest, giddy, like a summation of waves crashing through his body. He forgot the small problem of handing Claudio in, and turned to Gigi. She leaned in and they held each other before she ushered him back to the restaurant, Nicola reluctant to let go.

"Go." she said, smiling.

He walked back inside, his creased shirt catching Petra's eye.

"Oooh, Nicola.." she said, blowing him kisses.

"Never mind that. Where's Claudio?"

"He left. Said he'll see you soon. What happened with Gina?"

"Gigi happened." He smiled and sat down.

"Back to Gigi now are we?" said Petra, clapping her hands.

"Dad left me a letter to read after he died. He hoped that all was not lost with Gigi. He called her that too."

"He loved that girl," said Sia. "And so do we. You won't get better. She's a treasure. That hair of hers is the eighth natural wonder of the world."

Nicola tried to stay calm as he drove home. Claudio's car was gone. Inside, His room was empty, the bed made. He drove to Claudio's house and cursed as light after light went red against him in synchronised fashion. He parked and was relieved to see Claudio's front door open.

Nicola knocked and walked in. The fumes were still strong. Claudio called out from the kitchen. "In here."

"What are you doing?"

"I wanted to air the place out. I wanted to leave it clean and fresh for whoever lives here. I am going to rent it out until, well, until. What happened with the girl?"

"We're going to try again."

Claudio screwed his face up in disgust. "Try again? Do better than try. Marry her."

"How did you want to do this?"

"I don't want any fuss. Can you walk me into the police station, Nicola? I don't want to be alone when I give myself in."

Nicola dry retched and had to sit down. Claudio made him a small drink.

He took a small sip and his mouth burned. His body warmed in seconds and his eyes wanted to close. "What is this?"

"Shh… drink it. There is too much on your plate Nicola. Lidia, me, your wife...yes you will marry her. Because if you don't, I will break out of prison and make sure you do."

"*Salute.*" They clinked glasses. Nicola sipped the rest of the *grappa divina* and soon pepped up. They shared one last coffee and got in the car. The drive went too fast for

Nicola. They were passing over the Bolte Bridge and heading for St Kilda Road.

"All the times we shared Nicola; they are up here. I love you like my son. Don't worry about me. I have lived a good life. All you owe me is to have one as well."

He parked and rang Zivkovic to come to the main reception. They went into an interview room where Nicola explained everything. He hugged his uncle and cried while his uncle remained stoic. Outside the room, Zivkovic looked at Nicola with a stern expression.

"When did you realise and why didn't you tell me?"

"About two days-"

"What the fuck?"

"I buried my Mother today Stefan, so please, don't break my balls. After Ivan beat Gabriella pretty bad, Claudio took her in. Ivan tracked her to his house, but Claudio didn't let him in. How he found Ivan I don't know, but Claudio killed him to protect her from more abuse. Not a justification, but that's what happened. When I confronted Claudio with it, he confessed and offered no resistance."

"How?"

"Two things. Gabriella looks like Claudio's wife Morena. She passed from cancer in her late thirties. The age difference was too much for her, and he accepted they would not be together. But he could not trust Ivan to not leave her alone once he passed."

"And the second?"

"My Mother had dementia and brain cancer that returned. About two weeks ago, she murmured in her sleep about how Claudio threw a man into the ocean for talking to her. Claudio was an intensely protective man."

Zivkovic wondered how many times he protected someone in the past.

"I understand and my condolences for your Mother. I'll note it on the report that he handed himself in. As for you, when do you want to come back? You're more than ready."

Nicola's head hurt and he squeezed his eyes tight.

"I'm going to need some time. I don't want some latent, PTSD type episode derail me again."

"Appreciate the honesty. Don't leave it too long though. After this, upstairs will be impressed with you. Well done. And look after yourself."

82

At ten, Nicola frothed milk for Gigi's cappuccino. She liked it lava hot, something he never understood. He smiled at the sound of her knock and ran to the door. Her hair was wild and free, her smile parabolic again. He ran his index finger over her smile.

"Hmm..$y = x^2$. The perfect parabola."

"What? Not that again."

She kissed him on the lips as she walked in. "I brought you some goodies."

They sat and sipped their coffees with the ricotta cannoli. Gigi turned to Nicola.

"Look, I don't want to waltz in here and pretend nothing's wrong. I need to explain what happened. Without that, this can't work, and it has to work."

"It does. I'm all ears."

She recounted in great detail the death of her baby sister Despina, twenty-two. She was on the way home from work. Her Mother rang her to bring home some groceries she had forgotten. Gigi offered to go but her Mother insisted that Despina get it on her way home. Despina made an illegal U-turn to get back to the supermarket, lost control, and oversteered into oncoming traffic. The

driver of the SUV was injured but Despina died at the
scene as the SUV caught her head on. The SUV driver
had an alcohol reading of 0.04, but it was Despina who
was at fault. Her Mother went into depression and her
Father shut down completely. Gigi held things together
for everyone but had to leave her job as her parents'
demands both practical and behavioural stretched her
limits. Relatives were either useless or gave the wrong
kind of help. She became sick more often and took
longer to recover. Her sleep was broken and often
punctuated by random crying from her parents' bedroom.
Her Father began wailing from his bedroom where he
spent his days, pining after her favourite daughter. His
Mother walked around in a constant twilight and said
nothing.

Four months later, her Mother suffered a heart attack.
After stabilising with a stent, she died of a stroke a
month later. As she tried to keep it all together, her
Father became incapacitated with a stroke of his own,
rendering him dependent on her for everything. Gigi
found the mountain of looking after him too high. She
sold the family home and moved him into a home for
stroke care. She moved into a flat in Moonee Ponds, five
minutes away from him. She lost all contact with people
and only left the flat to visit her Father and, for her
weekly psychiatrist appointment in Essendon. As her
Father's condition worsened, they fought when she
visited him. One day, she experienced a panic attack that
left her left side paralysed. She was hospitalised, then
booked into Thomas Embling Hospital in Fairfield,
where she spent two months recuperating. After many

false alarms, her Father passed in his sleep, he too from a heart attack. As the only first degree relative, she bore the brunt of a third funeral in a year. She endured countless visits and advice from people who knew everything and nothing. A sense of freedom came at the wake after the last relative left the church hall, but tragedy had worn her thin. Her body shut down and basic decisions became convoluted, her life a haze. She returned to Thomas Embling and took four months to recover any degree of balance in her life. H gave her Nicola's card after suggesting some cognitive therapy. She made the one clear decision she had made since the wake.

"That day I came in was about three months after my Father's funeral, Nicola. After my Father's funeral, my mind turned to you many times, but I thought too much time had passed. When Alex told me your name, I had to see you, even though I knew you would be angry. I was prepared to face you."

"I'm sorry, Gigi." Nicola cried as she absorbed her tragedy. He bowed his head and found it hard to look her in the eye. "After all that, you still showed up that day and took my abuse. I hurt you."

"Look at me, Nicola. You need to look at me. Good. Stay with me. I can tell you're sorry. You weren't aware of all this. You have gone through your own version of hell."

"I want you to meet someone. Come with me," he said. He texted Alex to meet him. As they walked into the café across from the clinic, Gigi looked at Nicola. "What are we doing here?"

"Here's Alex now." Gigi went pale.

Alex kissed her hello and sat next to her. "What is going on?" asked Gigi, her face contorted in horror.

"Alex is my half-sister. Nectarios is our Dad. He had a thing with Alex's Mother before I was born."

"Oh my God, Nicola, you scared the Jesus out of me."

Alex screwed up her face and laughed. "You thought that... oh God no, that would be weird."

"Very." said Nicola.

Claudio pleaded guilty to the charge of murder. He asked for his sentencing to happen as soon as possible. Nicola sat with Gabriella as they heard proceedings. Claudio did not turn and made sure he did not make eye contact with either of them as he was led away.

Nicola helped Gigi move in. She wanted to leave the area west of Sydney Rd behind. West of this line defined a zone of tragedy on a map in her mind; Waverley Road where her sister died, John Fawkner hospital and her Father's nursing home. She wanted it all in the past.

Nicola gave her free reign over where her things went. *La donna è la chiave della casa*, Lidia used to say. The woman is the key to the house. Nicola decided to move into his parents' larger bedroom. It had the ensuite with dual vanity units and was far more practical for Gigi and her hair. Nicola's bedroom became a study for them both and they rearranged the living area. Apart from the few trips away, they hadn't lived together. They were hesitant about each other's space, with the occasional 'no after you' that all couples went through.

They settled into their domestic bliss, learning how to live in each other's space. Nicola cooked until Gigi insisted that they cook together while time allowed. They cleared the back garden, which. while small, was overgrown with ivy, Nectarios' sworn enemy. They enjoyed the sweat and the sense of achievement. Gigi began looking for work again, a step Nicola encouraged. H implored him to return for three half-day sessions a week as many still asked after him. He began seeing patients again but found himself irritated by the end of his sessions. Alex sat in his chair and leant forward.

"You Ok?"

"Yeah. fine."

"You sure?"

"Juggling all these balls at once was easier. Now life is less congested, I rush over things I don't need to."

"No time to think when your brain is occupied. You didn't get time to grieve when Dad passed away. Now you're grieving for both your Mum and Dad."

Nicola's head hurt at the realisation. "You're right, you're so right."

"Are you sleeping Ok? Is Gigi taking the doona?"

"She doesn't sleep, she purrs. I'm sleeping but I'm tired all the time."

"H would kill me if he heard this, but a holiday wouldn't hurt."

"True."

Nicola considered taking a holiday as selfish before. Now nothing held them back. He sat with Gigi and they looked at Italy and Greece. No one else depended on them. They were either dead or incarcerated. They agreed to a month in Italy, working top to bottom. At two in the morning, they were getting nowhere with all the options and were both tired and distracted. They decided to start fresh the next day. The urgency edged off and they decided to just enjoy being together at home for a while.

The forty days since Lidia's passing came. They observed it with a picnic by her side, warm until the sun dove behind the afternoon clouds. They walked back home through Curtain Park. A boy followed his older sister along the winding concrete path on skateboards. The boy became jealous at his sister's superior balance and tried to overtake her. Nicola moved out of his way onto the grass. He toppled over and fell sideways, landing on his shoulder. Children played in the distance on the merry go round and the skateboards grated over the concrete. Then the sky began turning. Gigi thought he tripped before she knelt over him and saw his eyes rolling back into his head. She felt him and confirmed a temperature. She called an ambulance and kept him comfortable. *I can't move my neck* he said to Gigi in the ambulance, his voice muffled through the oxygen mask, his eyes wide in confusion and fear. She rubbed his forearm and calmed him before his body convulsed, shoulders jerking, the metal bed rattling. The paramedic cleared the space around him. It persisted for an agonising five minutes. His chest rose and fell and Gigi tried to relax for Nicola's sake.

In an assessment room in Royal Melbourne Hospital, he lay limp, his rest punctuated by blood tests and scans. The nurses sent Gigi home after she stayed all night, saying it was for her own good. She complied, but after three hours of pacing the house front to back, she returned. The nurse who sent Gigi home put a blanket over her legs as she slept with her feet on a chair.

> *Nicola woke, aged twelve. A younger Lidia stood at the foot of his bed. She looked over his chart: Nicola, calma figlio, she said; be calm, boy. He closed his eyes and open them to see Lidia now older, transparent and hovering before getting into a small wooden boat. She floated away and out the door with a peaceful face. Nectarios rowed slow and cooed to her. 'Before you slip into unconsciousness..'*

A doctor approached Gigi, a waif-like woman with sprawling hair like hers. She rubbed her shoulder.

"Mrs Petrakis?"

"Ah no, I'm his girlfriend. What's happening?"

"Nicola has encephalitis, most likely a herpes virus. He was here twelve years ago with Shingles. Has he been under stress lately?"

"You could say that. Family stress, bereavements."

"We're putting him on intravenous Acyclovir straight away, as well as an anticonvulsant. As the antiviral kicks in his temp will drop and we won't have any more seizures. He was frying when he came in: 40.4 degrees."

"How long will he be here?"

"Minimum seven, ten days."

They moved Nicola to another room at Royal Melbourne. He was able to stay awake long enough to be responsive on the third day, but even the shortest of conversations taxed him and his temperature proved difficult to lower. The day after his third year Uni exams, he was ambushed by shingles. Records of his hospitalisation at Royal Melbourne made the diagnosis easier.

The Acyclovir in his system, his temperature began to drop. He still experienced spikes and frightening vignettes flashed through his brain.

> *The humidity in the greenhouse was stifling. The snakes were coming from every gap in the dense hedge and soon covered the mossy floor. Like Indiana Jones. Claudio handed him a flaming torch and vanished. The snakes lunged and he waved fire at them. He grabbed one and lit its tail as his torch dwindled down to his hand. Surprised it took flame, he used it to ward off the others.*

> *Gigi sat on Port Melbourne pier, legs dangling, toes just covered by the lapping water. The high waves roared in from Bass Strait. The two girls in their teens ran down to her, the boards echoing and their black hair trailing behind. They tried to*

He gasped for air each time he woke from a dream, only
to fall asleep again and be forced through another one.
Gigi saw the fright in his face each time he woke and
made a playlist for him to try and replace the demons
playing in his head. It helped him settle and the dreams
stayed under the radar. He demanded more blankets and
shivered through the night until day five when he
stabilised below 38 degrees.

Nicola asked Gigi to put the song he was listening to on
repeat. He loved *Lloyd Cole and The Commotions*
growing up. He sang 'Perfect Blue' with closed eyes, but
now it sounded like a new song.

I dream the ocean was in my house
I feel the surf against my skin
But I just can't keep the waves from dragging me down
But when you say

Ooh, baby, you're my best friend
Then I lose I lose my common sense
I'm kind of blue it's the truth

He sang the words out loud. Gigi smiled, then cried.
By day six he could sit up and talk without getting tired.
Gigi and Alex sat with him and poked fun. Alex brought
in Rena the next day. She demanded to see him and bring
in more roast lamb for him. His appetite returned and he
cleared the plate, giving himself hiccups. From her bag,
she removed a jar of *vanilia*, a thick vanilla mastic paste
and a spoon. Nicola's eyes lit up and looked at Rena.

"How did you know?"

"Nectarios told me that Lidia couldn't stand the smell but
when he came to my house, we enjoyed it in secret."

Nicola scooped two large spoonful's and rested them in a
glass of cold water, just like he did when he visited Sia.
He finished the jar before he left hospital. The
encephalitis had taxed his body, and he left a stone
lighter than when he arrived, despite the *vanilia* binge.

85

Claudio dressed for his sentencing. The guards found him easy to manage, like many older men incarcerated for the first time. They knew how the world worked. They led him into the van and into court. Claudio looked and could not see Nicola. Gabriella arrived late and sat at the very back after the judge came in. Judge Acaster, a burly man with an impressive walrus moustache, looked at Claudio and raised his hand as a signal to stand. His voice sounded rough, but with the rhythm of a seasoned orator.

"Claudio Liverani, I could begin with your journey to where you stand now, but what is clear that you premeditated to murder Ivan Constantin in his garage. In your testimony, you wanted to protect a woman he was abusive to. You committed this murder to keep her safe once you were gone. The instinct and wish to protect someone from harm is admirable, but you crossed the line from protection to inflict your own abuse. That you chose such brutal means to end this man's life is unforgivable. While Ivan Constantin was a loan shark, dealt in stolen goods, dealt drugs and prone to violence, there were laws to punish him. Others exist to punish the taking of human life. You premeditated to murder Mr Constantin, to cause him unimaginable pain and suffering in the moments before he died. Before I sentence you, do you have anything to tell the court?"

Claudio stood and gripped the table for balance.

"Your Honour, I thank the court for making this process quick. I do not apologise for protecting the woman we are speaking about. I do not ask for a lower sentence because of this. In fact, I ask you to give me a life sentence without parole. I had a heart attack one month before I killed this man. I am certain that I will die in jail before any sentence you deliver is over. I will die happy that this woman will be safe, at least from him."

Judge Acaster weighed up his decision.

"Mr Liverani, I sentence you to life imprisonment without parole."

He looked around as the bailiffs led him away to see Gabriella leaving.

86

By day ten, the doctors on the ward were happy that the infection was under control. Nicola could go home with oral Acyclovir. Dr Shahidi, a neurologist, shouted down the phone at the ward doctor for not requesting a neurological assessment before discharge.

"Napoleon's on his way," said the ward doctor to his colleague.

The doctors stood against the wall as Napoleon completed the bollocking in person for Nicola's benefit.

"So, his temperature's down, his vitals sorted - let's send him home without a seizure management plan."

"He only suffered a seizure in the acute phase, Iqbal."

"It's Doctor Shahidi to you. Get a fresh MRI done now. My apologies Mr Petrakis."

The images sat side by side on Dr Shah's screens an hour later. While the frontal lobe lesions defining the infected areas were gone, but residual areas of swelling remained in the temporal lobe. These suggested the risk of ongoing seizures. He placed him on two prophylactic anti-epileptic drugs and advised stress management. Gigi brought him home later that morning. She made a stash of meals to make life easier. She reheated some carbonara and looked at him with a wink.

"Welcome home, my boy."

"Thank you, Gigi. This life is a killer isn't it?"

"You're not going anywhere. You're going to be fine."

"There was a moment, I can't remember what day, where I thought I was dying."

"I would kill you if you died on me now. So much to do."

"Now I'm the burden. I could have a seizure at any time. Still happy to fight with me?"

"You're on drugs to stop them. Stressing isn't going to help. We'll fight more when you're better." She raised her fists and led with the left before delivering a pretend right jab.

Nicola's eyes drooped after lunch and Gigi walked him off to bed. He looked at the ceiling and his mind wandered to Lidia's drawer. He held up Lidia's white gold ring and wondered if it would fit. He put it on his own finger and played the light over the aquamarine stone set on its flatter curve. Lidia had brought it over from Italy, her favourite piece. He slid it up and down his ring finger. *A slight resizing down* he thought. Gigi's fingers were slenderer than Lidia's. He woke around dinner time or what looked like dinner time. He couldn't be sure. They ate a light salad and watched *As Good As It Gets*. Nicola laughed as Jack Nicholson delivered the title line in the psychiatrist's waiting room. He realised that sitting in a lounge room with your loved one was as good as it gets.

The movie long finished, some Canadian couple in Tuscany searched for a flat in some cringeworthy reality show. Gigi fell asleep on the couch. Nicola crept across the floor and slipped the ring on her finger. The ring fit better than he thought. She laughed at the tickling of him turning the ring the right way up. She rubbed her thumb against her fingers, felt the ring and sat up with a shriek, looking wide-eyed from the ring to Nicola.

"Not a great proposal but we must get married, Gigi."

She looked at the ring and cried. "I'm yours Nicola, ring or no ring." She kissed him. They held each other for a few minutes until Gigi spoke into his ear.

"I'd like a special day, but no overblown wedding, or maybe just a dinner here."

"Whatever Gigi wants."

"This ring is gorgeous!"

"It was Lidia's, from Italy. She would want you to have it."

Gigi began crying, a sad cry.

"What's wrong?"

"I always thought when this happened that I would call Desi. She's not there."

"I know," he said, wiping her cheeks. "You will always feel her with you."

She nodded and apologised.

"Shh- no need to apologise. Enjoy it with me."

They trod off to bed and lay staring at the ceiling. Gigi turned to him.

"So, how many do you want?"

"Probably about seven."

"That many?"

"Well I don't it to be a circus."

"What are we talking about here?"

"Seven guests, something small."

"What guests, I was talking about kids you banana."

"Kids? Of course, I want kids. Two, maybe three would be nice."

"If I told you I couldn't have kids would you stay with me?"

"Of course. What a stupid question."

She sat up. "Why is that such a stupid question? Things change and I need to know where you stand."

Nicola squeezed her hand and kissed it. "Nothing will change how I feel. I promise you this."

Her face broke into a smile and she moved his hand to her stomach. "That's just as well. I'm pregnant."

The room spun. Nicola moaned *oh no* and reached out for Gigi's hand. She grabbed hard and told him to close his eyes. She kissed him hard on the forehead and whispered *Hello Daddy*. He cried with giddy laughter. They slept in.

87

Claudio adapted well to prison life. He recognised and embraced the discipline. His crime ranked as a 'good' crime in the hierarchy of crimes amongst inmates. Some of the younger ones gravitated towards his warm uncle persona. Nicola promised he would visit when he handed him over to Zivkovic. After four weeks, he came. Claudio didn't resent his nephew and was happy when he did.

"Have you been Ok, Zio?"

"They treat me well here. I'm the model inmate. I prefer that to prisoner."

"Has Gabriella come in?"

"Not yet, but she will when she is ready. What happened to you? You have lost some weight. Are you sick? Is that why you haven't come?"

"I was." he explained.

"I'm not surprised," Claudio said. "All that stress and worrying, it has to go somewhere. And the girl?"

"She said yes." He held up his left hand and showed the titanium engagement ring Gigi bought for him.

Claudio kissed his nephew on the forehead and nodded in approval. "Good boy, congratulations. She is a lovely girl. Make babies together, fill that house and replace the sadness."

Nicola smiled. Claudio clapped his hands together in joy.

"*Minchia*. Didn't waste time, did you?"

"We're not young, Zio."

The guard had allowed Claudio an extra ten minutes but now he signalled to wrap it up.

"Nicola, you are all I have as family. I wish you a happy life, my boy." He cried as he hugged him. He backed away and focused on Nicola until he turned out of sight.

Gabriella came two days later. They sat opposite each other, neither sure of what to say or how to act. Gabriella whispered thank you to him. He smiled back.

"Are you well? You look well."

"I'm Ok. Are they treating you well here? How's the food?"

"Gabriella, I am fine in every sense. I am at peace knowing you will be safe."

Gabriella held his hand.

"I didn't ask you to-"

"Shh - *I* made that decision. You have nothing to be sorry for. Are you working?"

"I changed jobs, Claudio. I'm working at a florist."

"A beautiful flower arranging flowers." he laughed.

She allowed herself to smile. "Yes, I enjoy it very much. I used to help my Zia."

The conversation dried up. Gabriella got up and kissed Claudio goodbye.

"You are not obliged to visit me, Gabriella. You will meet a man; time will be less. I understand. I wish you well."

For the second time, Gabriella had the impression of Claudio drawing a line between them, like a final goodbye, a dread she couldn't shake. Back in his cell, Claudio sat before a picture of Morena tacked to the wall. *Ti vedo subito*. It won't be long, Morena. In prison, Claudio kept to himself, read and watched TV, but the boredom would finish him, he thought. He had paid for doing what he thought and believed was right. He stopped taking his heart tablets and anticoagulants and waited for death to come. After a few days, his breathing became heavy, but it wouldn't come. He resisted the temptation to restart his tablets and waited through the lethargy, time slowing to a crawl. After three days of stasis and willing the attack to take him, he began feeling clammy and a dull pain flared across his left shoulder. He took four sleeping tablets and lay down with Morena's picture on his pocket. As his body made its final contractions, the picture slid onto the bed beside him. The guard found him unresponsive in the morning. The prison doctor pronounced him dead after repeated attempts at CPR.

88

Nicola cried when contacted as the next of kin, then numbness from all the grieving. He collected Claudio's belongings. Claudio had requested no funeral service but instead to be cremated and his ashes to be spread over Morena's grave. Nicola accompanied his body to the funeral home and went home to open the box with his belongings. In it was his watch, rings, cross and chain, and a letter addressed to him written in Italian.

Dear Nicola

Thank you for carrying out my wishes. I am not sure if Morena will be where I am going but I have hopes. She loved you even though you were only five when she died. She called you Nicoluccio. But that was a long time ago. I knew my time was coming and did not want too many loose ends for you to worry about. After all, you have a wedding and a baby coming! But the truth is that since your Zia left this earth, I have been a nomad waiting to die, but I am grateful to have had you with me. We have fished together, hunted together and argued together. And now there is no more.

I do not regret what I did to that figlio di minchia that hurt Gabriella. In Taormina, a man joked about having his way with your Mother. She was 18. I knocked him out and threw him into the Strait of Messina, down a cliff.

On the boat, I left your Mother alone for a minute, and I came back to see a man with his hands inside her dress. She didn't encourage him. She was a natural beauty and attracted men wherever she went. I threw him into the sea about a day after we passed through the Suez Canal. Your Mother told the captain that she had seen a man drinking. These bastardi deserved to die. At fourteen years of age, I caught a priest in my town molesting a girl not yet ten. I interrupted them. I struck his head with a rock and killed him.

Nicola picked up the card at the bottom of the box for a solicitor not far from Iain Grafton's office. He found himself again involved in a will. Adam Di Fazio was a young-looking man of average height. Only a few grey hairs pointed to him having any experience. Nicola read through the will.

"Looks pretty straightforward."

"He wanted a very simple will. Call me if you have any questions."

89

Two days later, Nicola stood with Gigi and Gabriella at Morena's grave. Located on the opposite side of the cemetery to Lidia and Nectarios, established trees protected it from gusts of wind. Gabriella asked to scatter the ashes. She dusted them from the head of the grave to the foot, spreading the rest at the base of the headstone. She handed the urn back to Nicola. They stayed for another minute, then walked back to his house. Gigi suggested they avoid Curtain Park, but Nicola insisted they walk through, walking past the exact spot where his brain exploded. He closed his eyes and enjoyed hearing the sound of kids playing in the distance. *Our kids will do the same* he whispered to Gigi. He looked forward to many days of sitting on the grass here, watching their kids become his and Gigi's clocks.

Nicola made them coffee.

"I'm glad this boy saw sense, Gigi." said Gabriella.

"So's he."

"Gabriella, Claudio left you something in the will."

"Sorry?"

"Claudio left you his house in Coburg." The house was all paid off and hers. She put her hands up in protest. "I can't. No. Sorry, Nicola."

"It's yours Gabriella."

"Are you sure?"

"Claudio can't hear you. He left you a letter too. Here."

She took her time and sighed. "OK."

"Don't be embarrassed or awkward. Not that my opinion should matter, but I am fine with the decision - if that makes the decision easier for you."

"It does."

It took a week to complete the paperwork. They met at the house. Gabriella shielded her eyes as the wind kicked up dust.

"Are you sure you don't begrudge me this?"

"It's not mine to begrudge and no I don't. Have a look at your house," said Nicola, handing her the keys.

The house was pristine and no longer reeked of fumes. Their conversation echoed in the emptiness.

"He planned all this didn't he?"

"Claudio always planned everything."

She walked through and marvelled at the size of the rooms and the possibilities. She heard the train in the distance. Morena's portrait sat above Claudio's bed. It didn't intimidate her like it did the first time she saw it.

"When are you thinking of moving in?"

"I can't fill this house, Nicola. I'm actually thinking of moving to Italy."

"Really?"

"I always wanted to live in Sicily. My parents came from Siracusa. I went at fourteen with them and I loved it. I got my Italian passport last week after eighteen months."

"That quick? You must know someone in the consulate."

She laughed.

Gabriella sold the house at auction four weeks later. In a hot housing market, the thirty-day settlement she requested posed no issue. After a heated duel, it went for $1.2 million. She began researching rentals in Siracusa.

90

Nicola and Gigi waited. The obstetrician was running later than usual, and they had exhausted the magazines. Gigi nestled her head into Nicola's chest and closed her eyes.

"Have we thought about names?"

"We don't know the sex yet."

"Gina Liakos." called out Renee De Marche.

"How are we?"

"Sick around the clock."

"Great, great news." She applied the gel to the probe and rubbed at various angles. Nicola read concern in De Marche's face as she zigged and zagged the probe at various angles. She struggled to see or hear anything. Five minutes passed and Gigi clung at the sides of the chair. De Marche cleaned the probe and reapplied gel three times, but nothing showed.

"Where is it?" cried Gigi,

"Shh, relax. It's playing hide and seek." said De Marche, holding her hand.

A beep, and then the squelch-squelch of the heartbeat. "There we go," said De Marche. She still looked concerned though, and after adjusting Gigi's position, she reapplied the gel and started again. "Hello, you," De Marche said. The sounds were indistinct now, and both Nicola and Gigi looked at each other in confusion. De Marche clicked the keyboard in what looked like a random manner, her hands whizzing from the roller ball to the keys and back. She collected the printouts with one hand and moved the probe with the other. After three more clicks, she rubbed the probe clean and handed Gigi some tissues.

"Do twins run in either of your families?" She held up the two clearest images and gave them one each. Nicola remembered his Thia Rita. She got them up on the screen and smiled at them as she held them up. "Say hello to your twins."

They both took a sharp intake of breath and looked at each other, mute, stunned.

Nicola recovered first. "Are they healthy?"

"So far, so good. I estimate them as eight, nine weeks old. They're close together in dimension and both have a strong heartbeat. Strap in beautiful people, you're going to be seeing a lot of me."

"You're absolutely sure of this?" said Gigi. She rubbed her abdomen, still in shock.

"The camera doesn't lie." said De Marche.

De Marche's secretary handed them the list of appointments and wished them congratulations. She pointed out the twins that De Marche had delivered. "You're in good hands."

Gigi looked from one set to another and felt nauseous. "Do you mind if we sit and rest for a little bit?"

"Go for it. It won't be the last time you ask."

As they sat, Gigi turned to a smiling Nicola. "Now you've done it haven't you?"

Nicola began to doze off.

> *The pier again, Gigi and the two girls, younger this time, the tide rising and the high, foaming waves coming toward them.*

Gigi prodded him and he woke with a start.

"You look like you've seen a ghost. You OK?"

"Nothing, I just drifted off."

"Ok pardner, let's go. I'm feeling better now but I need food."

Nicola drove home at a snail's pace, drawing the ire of drivers behind him.

"I'm protecting my family!" he yelled out, laughing.

91

Gabriella packed enough clothes for seven days and decided to buy herself a new wardrobe when she arrived. She confirmed her hotel bookings and ticked off all her list of loose ends. She left Tullamarine at eleven degrees and walked out of Fiumicino Airport to a warm twenty-nine. She enjoyed business class and felt no stiffness or cramping as she walked to collect her baggage.

She stayed in Rome for two nights, adopting the local time zone to defeat jet lag before taking a first-class cabin on a train to Palermo. She enjoyed the solitude of train journeys and found them intriguing. She used the time to brush up on her Italian, which sat between tourist and intermediate. She wanted to be quick on her feet in conversation and not be taken advantage of. Learning the dialect didn't concern her. That could come later.

She thought of Claudio often. She remembered the day he walked into the brothel, how his eyes locked onto hers; a cinder in snow's chance for her to be a doppelganger of his late wife. She shuddered when she thought how events cascaded to place her where she stood.

Morena's huge portrait posed a problem. Disposing of it was disrespectful to the memory of both Morena and Claudio. She took it to an art gallery on Brunswick Street, Fitzroy. A petite woman with red hair and heavy make-up only saw value in the enormous metal framing and tried to finalise a transaction with great haste. Her husband, an older man with a shock of white hair fell in love with it as he walked in. He insisted with great drama that it stay intact, his hair falling across his large, square face as he prosecuted his case.

The woman scoffed and waved a hand around the gallery, its walls full and space scarce. "Where do we have room to store this, Justin? Where?"

"Ignore her. I expect nothing more from a salvager's daughter. Does this look like a damaged car to you, Tina?" said the man to his wife.

"Here we go, always the drama," she responded, her eyes rolling under a mass of mascara.

Justin stood back and looked from the portrait to Gabriella.

"No no, it's a long story- it's not me. Her name is Morena."

"It may as well be. Exquisite. I'm-"

"Justin, I know. Gabriella. Nice to meet you. I'll be back in a while you and Tina can discuss. I trust you both to leave the painting intact. I'm moving overseas and can't take it overseas with me."

To Tina's irritation, Justin found the black hair and beauty of the face rendered in oil intoxicating. The couple fought before agreeing on a price and then fought again after Gabriella left. Justin wore being banished from the bedroom before Tina traded on his aroused state. One night she arrived home with jet black hair and took a shocked Justin to bed without a word.

Morena hung as a prominent display piece, seen by many eyes. The couple refused offers, many substantial.

Gabriella slept on a bed more generous than she expected on a train. It allowed her to sleep on either side and stretch her legs without any restriction. When she woke, her phone told her they were in Vibo Valentia, Calabria. She looked out the window and marvelled at the houses perched near the vertical cliff towering over the beach. The sun's reflection off the cliff face dazzled. All this she would see in good time. She had an early dinner in the restaurant cart. The sense of culture agreed with her; the intelligent conversations, the lack of pomposity with the food, the courtesy. Her well-trained antennae detected eyes moving over her. She ignored the looks from a group of men dining at the opposite end of the cart and declined their offer to join them. She woke at the jolt of the train rolling onto the ferry that carried it across to Messina. She walked up to the deck and saw the array of lights across the strait. The headland rolled down to the shore and in the dusk the land appeared to cradle the bay like a Mother's arm. In Messina she found her hotel, where she ran a bath and stretched out on a glorious king-sized bed. She made her train in good time after a sleep in and enjoyed the three-hour trip to Siracusa in bright sunshine.

92

Nicola was happy to hear from Olivia. She and Ben were in Melbourne for the weekend and wanted to catch up. They sat in a park in beautiful sunshine. Maya and Grace tormented poor Jeremy around the playground and up and down the grassed dunes.

When Nicola recounted the Kondos story to Gigi at home, she admonished him just as Alex had.

"How many weeks are you, Olivia?"

"Nearly twenty. You?"

"Just clocked fourteen."

Nicola frowned as he made the calculation in his head and jumped to the conclusion that all three babies sitting warm and snug in the women around him were his. He began to shake and sweat. *How long* thought Nicola. Six, maybe seven weeks before Gigi came back into his life? Olivia looked at him and winked. Nicola sweated some more. Gigi rubbed her abdomen and looked across the park. That their encounter happened before Gigi's second coming did nothing to calm him. Though he trusted Olivia, she could turn their world upside down in a sentence.

Nicola shifted on the grass and struggled to find a comfortable position. Gigi looked up at him.

"You're like a dog on a new bed. What's wrong, Nico?"

Nicola couldn't settle and got up to go for a walk.

"Yeah just a bit hot. I'll be back in a sec."

A minute later, Olivia's text message came through.

Not yours. Calm down FFS you idiot.
BTW she's beautiful. You two are great together.
Might wanna delete this message. x

Nicola sat on a bench away from the others and wiped the message from his phone. The breeze cooled him off and he exhaled. He jumped as Ben sat next to him,

"Funny thing fate isn't it?" said Ben

"Never a truer word spoken." said Nicola,

"When Adelina died, I resigned myself to it being me and Jeremy. For three years I convinced myself that I was happy. Then Olivia came along and turned everything on its head. We wanted a child of our own and here we are. We're calling it Nicola, whether it's a boy or a girl."

He looked across at Ben. "What?"

"If not for you, we would never have met. Bizarre circumstances, but like I said, fate. Now we're linked

forever." Ben put his arm around Nicola and left it there
for longer than Nicola was comfortable with.

The men returned and they all ate and relaxed with wine
well into the afternoon. Nicola didn't know what to think
about Olivia's baby being called Nicola. He hoped it was
a girl.

Gigi and Nicola stayed after Olivia and Ben left. Gigi lay
across his stomach when they got home later. Nicola
pulled gently at her hair, the coiled black strands falling
back into place as he released them.

"It's nice when you do that. When I did it, it was a
neurotic compulsion. Took me months to stop doing it,
so stupid."

"Are you ready, beautiful?"

"For what?" replied Gigi.

"All this."

"Nicola, we women are born ready." She stood up and
turned around, hands clasped around her belly. "Can we
please just get married while I can still find a wedding
dress I can fit into?"

"Might be a good idea." Nicola looked off across the
park. The tops of the trees dividing the eastern half of the
park whooshed as an afternoon change came through.

"Nico?"

"Yes, bella."

"What song is in your head now?"

"Ain't That A Kick in The Head."

"Dean Martin?"

"The one and only."

They walked home. Nicola put it on and danced Gigi around the dining table.

> *She's tellin' me we'll be wed,*
> *She's picked out a king-sized bed.*
> *I couldn't feel better, or I'd be sick*
> *Tell me quick, ain't that a kick?*
> *Tell me quick, ain't that a kick in the head?*

They booked a service after ringing every Orthodox Church in Melbourne, eventually securing a ceremony at The Presentation of Our Lady in North Balwyn. Alex and Petra dropped everything to help Gigi find a dress off the rack and sat with her as an Italian seamstress with hands gnarled from arthritis adjusted it for her. With the small gathering, the Priest agreed to shoehorn them in between a baptism and another wedding. They walked each other down the aisle as Petra, Sia, Alex and Rena sat in the front row.

The party of six had a late lunch at a winery near Yarra Glen, Petra took a photo of them in a boxing pose on the lush grass, Gigi's mock right cross perfectly meeting his chin with the afternoon sun lighting the mountains in the background. They had the photo blown up and placed on their study wall as a reminder to never stop fighting,

93

Gabriella neared the end of her short-term lease. In the six weeks she had stayed in the pokey one bedroom flat in the east area of Siracusa, she had seen over twenty apartments for sale. She shortlisted three, but one grabbed her heart. Although dark and unappealing to the eye, Gabriella saw great opportunity in its large space, and it had sole access to a rooftop area with a small garden, a clothesline and a view to the ancient city of Ortigia across the bay. The previous owner had given up renovating, the works stopping after painting the walls and replacing the floors. He ran out of money and wanted to get what he could. At 145,000 euro, it was the most expensive of the three, but it allowed Gabriella to make it her own without excessive works. She made an offer of 110,000. They settled on 120,000 after she offered a thirty-day settlement and a fifty percent deposit. She also negotiated access to have a local young female architect come in and draw up her vision. Andrea Sipala recently left her firm and started her own business. Gabriella and Sipala talked over coffee, which bled into late evening. By midnight, they had a shared vision of the new apartment and were both excited.

"Proprio non hai peli sulla lingua, Gabriella. Una buona qualità d'avere in Sicilia," said Sipala in admiration of her first major client.

Gabriella loved the everyday Italian idioms. Not having any hairs on her tongue would indeed get her far here.

The works took four months from Sipala's drawings to completion. They became close friends and Sipala showed Gabriella the best spots to eat, shop and visit between renovations. She liked the final result very much. The dining and living areas flowed into the kitchen, where she spent hours cooking. She did a course in Sicilian cooking and soon became proficient, especially at pasta with squid ink, which she ate often. The minutiae of everyday life filled the gaps in her grasp of tenses and conjugation. The Siracusano dialect became easier to understand, but she still spoke in proper Italian out of respect, wary of coming across as a tourist trying to pass herself off as a local.

Claudio's letter stared at her on the fridge door, held by a magnet. She had avoided reading it till now but she had put it off too long.

> *Bella Gabriella*
> *Live well wherever you go.*
> *Look after yourself. There is only one of you.*
> *Sempre in tuo debito,*
> *Claudio*

She read the letter three times and kept it as a reminder. *Always in your debt* said the letter. *No, I am in your debt* she said to herself. After three months in her renovated apartment, a jitteriness in her stomach ate at her. It made her walk the streets to see what it was. She walked across the bridge to Ortigia and stood at the Fonte Arethusa after lunch. She read the plaque and smiled at the story. Arethusa, the nymph changed by the Goddess Artemis into a watercourse to escape the unwanted advances of a suitor, Alpheus.

Gabriella stood in front of the sculpture that depicted the scene. An old man broke from his wife and turned to her. His fisherman's moustache hid a big smile.

"La storia è strana, ma per noi è romantica. È rimasta per sempre una parte dell'istoria."
The story is strange, but for us it is romantic. She remains forever part of our history.

He might be right, she thought and smiled at the man.

She responded.

"Ma non è meglio esistere come acqua che essere umani e sentire emozioni?"
Is it better to exist as water or as a human who feels emotions?

The old man shrugged.

"Forse hai ragione signorina."
Maybe you're right.

After three hours of aimless walking, a sign on a florist shop caught her eye in central Siracusa.

Si vende, chiedete dentro.
For Sale, inquire within.

She rested her feet at the cafe across the street and watched for an hour. Eight people went in. Three left with flowers, the slow trade belying the busy passing foot traffic. For the first time, she thought in Italian.

Qualcosa non va.
Something is amiss.

The husband spoke as she entered. His dialect sounded more Calabrese than Siciliano. She made a gentle enquiry about how long they had been there. Gabriella soon gathered that the man and his wife came to help his close friend out while he battled cancer.

"Ten years ago," said the wife, holding up all ten fingers. "Now we are stuck with this fucking place and cannot sell it." She tried not to sound bitter, but in true Calabrese style, facts were facts.

"Sarina-"

"È la verita, no?"
It's true, no?

Gabriella looked around and a quick scan told her the couple traded on their goodwill as nice people but had little idea about floristry. She scanned the small shop and saw opportunity in the drab arrangements and dull lighting. It was in a great location, near the commercial area and its cafes. Both the *Ospedale Humberto* and Siracusa's public hospital, the *Azienda Sanitaria*

Provinciale, were within walking distance. It was also close by foot to her apartment on *Corso Timoleonte.*

"Quanto volete?" she asked.
How much?

The wife grabbed her husband's arm and dragged him into the back area and said. *"Ci scusate un pó "* The couple tried speaking in hushed voices, but Gabriella clearly caught them on the hop.

"Posso tornare in cinque minuti se avete bisogno di piú tempo." she shouted to them.
 I can come back in five if you need more time.

"No, no signorina. Tranquilla, ne parliamo." Relax, we can talk said the man through the curtain.

"Sapete qualcosa. Ceniamo stasera a casa mia e ne parliamo."
We'll talk over dinner at my house Gabriella said. They came out from the curtain and smiled.

"Crediamo che non ci stai prendendo per culo?" said the wife.
You're not having a lend of us, are you?

"Certamente no." Gabriella replied, and left her address and a time on her card.

She extended her hand. "Gabriella."

"Rino e Sarina. Piacere."

Gabriella made her pasta and squid ink. The couple
arrived and marvelled at the apartment. After dinner,
they negotiated. Their urgency lay in not having seen
their two children for three years. They had two young
grandchildren they were desperate to spoil. They
remained open seven days a week out of duty for their
now deceased friend. They swore on their friend's
memory that they would not return to Crotone until they
sold the business. That way they could return for good.
Their sense of duty at considerable personal loss stunned
and impressed Gabriella. However, she did not wish to
trade on their predicament for a good deal.

Gabriella tried not to appear shocked that they only
wanted 5,000 euro and for her to take over the remaining
18 months of the lease. The rent was a steal at 1100 euro
a month. She offered an extra 2,500 euro on the
condition they help her with a fortnight transition period.
They accepted with glee. Not wanting to be outdone,
they gave her the car they used for the business, an
ageing yet cute two-door red Fiat, her refusal drowned
out by their strong protestations. She negotiated the lease
to get a three-year term with an extension option for only
an extra 150 euro a month. She did business like a local.

By the end of the first week, she had enough faith in
herself to go it alone, even if the *burocrazia* gave her
kittens. She drove Rino and Sarina Saffrone to the train
station three days earlier than they agreed with tickets
she bought for them. She began refurbishing the shop, a

corner space, only thirty-five square metres. Gabriella repainted it in a weekend, after asking Andrea Sipala to source the exact pale azure to match the colour of the *mare Siracusa*. The white skirting boards made the space appear larger.

Located on Via Bacchilide, Gabriella renamed it *Fiori Bacchi* after the street and used the eagle of the city's crest as the logo. The bright exterior colours reminded locals that a florist existed. Business soon picked up. She negotiated contracts with the hospitals and attracted business from local offices. She paid a local brother and sister cash to deliver urgent orders. The one to three-thirty afternoon *pennichella* agreed with her, the short naps refreshing her for the late afternoon and evening trade, which picked up quicker than she expected.

As summer drew to a close, Gabriella frequented her private rooftop garden. She put a hammock and a large cantilever umbrella which she positioned according to the sun. The onshore wind had turned to the northeast and swung her like a baby. She looked over towards Ortigia and waited until her beautiful lights came on. She took another sip of her *Nero d'Avola*. Rino left her a plentiful stash of it with a note - *bonu vinu fa bonu sangu. Good wine makes good blood* indeed she thought. She kept the note on her fridge as a reminder next to Claudio's letter.

She thought of her place in the world. The journey lived up to its billing, but Gabriella found the concept of finally being at peace a fallacy. As grateful as she was for being safe and control of her destiny, the past and its vignettes persisted, finding moments in the day to intrude into the solitude. Her parents had passed long ago. The men who treated her well and those who had treated her mean were now one with the earth. She was her future until she decided to change it. That thought both scared and emboldened her. She breathed in the sea air and began to feel sleepy. The hammock rocked her in its gentle, shallow arc.

She looked across at Arethusa. She promised herself to make something of this life and not become a watercourse like Arethusa.

She raised a glass. *Buon anima, Claudio.*

94

Nicola slept in after writing reports well into the night. Gigi and the twins playing hide-and-seek inside her were taking up more of the bed, forcing Nicola to invent new sleeping positions. After the Ivan case, Zivkovic pestered him to come back, even on an ad hoc basis to interview and provide assessments. Ad hoc suited him just fine with the twins on the way. Human frailty and damaged psyches kept him busy. It also kept Alex and H off his back as he could flex his counselling up and down as the clinic demanded.

Gigi left early for work, having found a part-time position as a practice manager at a medium sized medical clinic. She gave animals a miss given her pregnancy. At seven months, she preferred starting early and being home by three p.m.

After teasing themselves about the sexes of their twins for months, the Scottish ultra-sonographer put them out of their misery and let it slip, thinking they already knew. Both Nicola and Gigi were over the concept of surprises and didn't mind.

They were having two girls and agreed to choose a name each. Despina and Ella were giving Gigi God awful reflux, with Nicola on hand with milk and peanut butter on toast. *Crunchy of course, only weirdos ate smooth* she said. Nicola put on the weight he lost in hospital back on during the pregnancy. Eating in solidarity agreed with

him. Alex claimed the role of Godmother for one and
Petra the other.

He took his coffee to the back veranda and sat. His head
turned at the sound of two lorikeets landing on the
railing. They edged with caution to the birdseed sculpture
that Gigi had hung. They settled on the ring around it and
pecked at the seeds. When they had their fill, they
perched on the railing and took turns nuzzling each other
clean.

The sun did their bright colours justice. Nicola smiled.